MEN
UNDER
WATER

DOUBLEDAY

NEW YORK
LONDON
TORONTO
SYDNEY
AUCKLAND

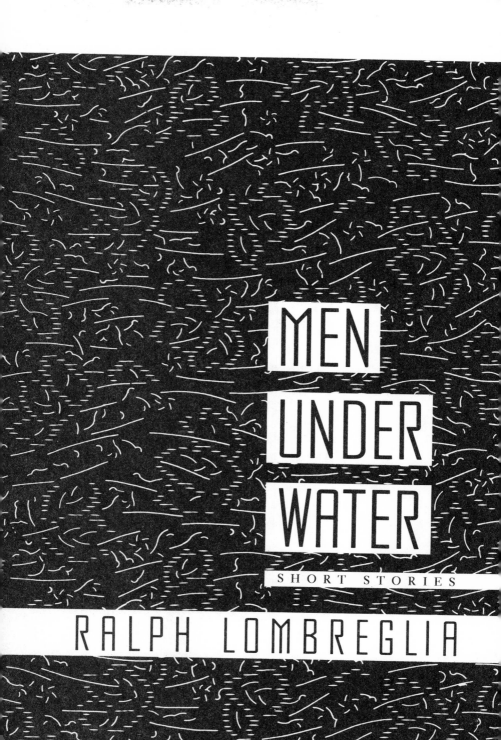

MEN UNDER WATER

SHORT STORIES

RALPH LOMBREGLIA

PUBLISHED BY DOUBLEDAY
a division of Bantam Doubleday Dell Publishing Group, Inc.
666 Fifth Avenue, New York, New York 10103

DOUBLEDAY and the portrayal of an anchor with a dolphin
are trademarks of Doubleday, a division of Bantam Doubleday
Dell Publishing Group, Inc.

Some of the stories in this collection originally appeared in
the following magazines, sometimes in slightly different form.
The author is grateful for permission to reprint.

The Atlantic: "Goodyear," "Men Under Water,"
"Inn Essence." *The New Yorker:* "Jungle Video."
The Iowa Review: "Museum of Love," "Jazzers."
Black Warrior Review: "Purification."

Library of Congress Cataloging-in-Publication Data

Lombreglia, Ralph.
   Men under water : short stories / Ralph Lombreglia.
— 1st ed.
      p.   cm.
   Contents: Inn essence — Goodyear — Museum of love
— Purification — Jazzers — Jungle video — Citizens —
Monarchs — Men under water.
   I. Title.
PS3562.O483M4   1990
813'.54—dc20   89-27428
                                                          CIP

ISBN 0-385-26335-X

For Doris and Ralph Sr.,
Larry, Donna,
Pat, and Cyndi.
And for Kate,
who helped make it.

Acknowledgments

The following institutions provided grants of money or time which helped to bring this book into being. The author is grateful for their generosity:

The Johns Hopkins University Writing Seminars, The Stanford University Writing Center, The National Endowment for the Arts, The New York Foundation for the Arts, The Corporation of Yaddo.

And special thanks to some true believers: C. Michael Curtis, Liz Darhansoff, David Gernert, Charles McGrath.

CONTENTS

MEN
UNDER
WATER

INN ESSENCE

For *a couple of months* here we had peace, relative peace, more peace anyway than you expect in the restaurant business. The occasion of this peace was the delivery of Victor, our pastry chef, to a mental hospital. He went there to recover from the breakdown he'd had in the kitchen one dark March afternoon. And even for a little while after Victor returned, things were good. He was taking his medication, his wife and kid were back from her mother's, he had a new life to think about. Once again he was in his own special zone of the kitchen making the most glorious chocolate desserts in the tri-state area. Some people say that Victor's creations go beyond culinary experience and into the realm of sex or voodoo. They say that on a good night finishing a meal at Inn Essence with the raspberry-laced chocolate torte or the Cointreau-bathed chocolate mousse is like having your body inhabited by the pastry chef himself.

Me, I try not to eat sweets, so I wouldn't know. But the point is, our peace is now gone. Victor has lost his mind again.

And for this reason I'm driving Route 80 east across northern New Jersey at 10:45 A.M., sleepy-headed in the right-hand lane, my blinker on for the exit that takes me to the restaurant. Forty miles more and I'd be on the George Washington Bridge, all of Manhattan lying before me like an antipasto tray. Right now I'd like to lean back and coast straight into it. At nine o'clock my telephone rang twice in rapid succession. I let the machine do its job, slept another hour, and then rolled out and listened to the messages. They were both from Jimmy Constanopoulos, my employer.

"Jeffrey," Jimmy said to me in the first message, *"my God, what a heartache this business is. Why are you working here, Jeffrey? You're a romantic, that's why. You think the restaurant business is romantic—don't deny it. I used to think that too. But now I'm a realist. I've had twenty years, I don't think I can take one more. Jeffrey, I've reconsidered our recent conversation. Go back and finish college. Get your degree. Yes, I said I wanted to groom you, turn you into a restaurateur. And I could do that. I could teach you to buy provisions, gain the trust of a staff, talk to the bank when the bank needed talking to. Manny could show you the famous veal medallions, the sauces that get written up in the papers. You already do beautiful salads. You could learn to mix a drink and hide cash from the registers at night. All the things I promised. But why, Jeffrey, why? So you could make*

*the same mistakes I made? You'd stay with me a few years,
I'd learn to love you like a son, and then the inevitable
would happen. You'd want your own place. Because you're
too smart to work for another man your whole life. You'd
come to me for help—a down payment, leverage with the
liquor-license people—and I wouldn't be able to turn you
down. I'd have to help you. And then your life would be
destroyed, like mine.*

"Jeffrey," Jimmy went on, *"I'm only going to say this
once. Don't ever—under any circumstances, no matter what
happens—even consider, for one minute, the idea of opening a restaurant."*

Jimmy hung up. And then the second message came on.

*"Jeffrey, I know you're there. Get over here right now. Yes,
I know, you're not on until three today. I'll make it up to
you. Victor just tried to kill one of the Thai students—the
little one, what's his name?—with a carving knife, no less.
He said they stole pastries from his walk-in. And then he
disappeared. Victor, I mean. I can't find him. And now the
Thai students won't come out of their house and work, and
I'm short-handed already, and we don't have enough desserts, and today is—what day is it, anyway? Christ, it's Friday. I've got to get my meat man on the phone. My bread
man. I've got to find Victor. Jeffrey, I won't forget the way
you've helped me. I'll set you up in business someday, you'll
have your own place. Just get over here and talk to the Thai
people. They like you. You're their friend."*

And then Jimmy hung up again.

Yes, I think to myself now, I could go for a day of hooky
in Nueva York. The bookstores, the theaters, the streets full
of people living lives of mysterious meaning. My foot wa-

vers between the brake and the gas. But then I think of the thousands of restaurants in Manhattan, five or six of them on every block, and I almost lose control of the car.

The day Victor got out of the mental hospital, Jimmy offered him a deal. If Victor would come back to work and make his brilliant desserts, take his tranquilizers, and behave himself, Jimmy would remodel the old carriage house in back of the restaurant, and Victor and his family could live in it free of charge. The desserts Jimmy had been buying in Victor's absence were like the shadows in Plato's cave, and this carriage house idea had a precedent—Manny the chef having occupied the place rent-free in the early days of Inn Essence.

Since then, true, it had fallen into wretched disrepair, lying empty or barely keeping rain off the heads of the assorted dishwashers and busboys Jimmy was forever trying to rehabilitate. I know, because I spent my own first month in its dank and peeling rooms. But the basic construction was the solid kind you don't see anymore, with enormous potential. He would put in skylights, Jimmy told Victor, and a working fireplace, a totally new kitchen and bath, and fresh paint on everything. He emphasized the old-fashioned gentility of it—the gifted chef-in-residence on the estate, waking with his wife to birdsong each morning, strolling to work through the woods like a country squire, fishing with his son at the stream when the day's desserts were done.

Victor came back to us a different man—quiet, productive, minding his own business, taking coffee breaks alone out back, where for a week or so, while Jimmy arranged for the carpenters to come, he could be seen staring past the dumpsters at the carriage house in a kind of reverie.

By this time it was late May, and one afternoon a red Mustang pulled up to Inn Essence. At the wheel was Kampon Padasha, an electrical-engineering student from Thailand. College was out now, and Kampon wanted a summer job. He came in and explained this to Ethel, our hostess, who was sitting at the bar smoking and sorting out credit-card receipts from the day before. She looked him over and nodded while he spoke. His English wasn't great. He was thin and gangly, not handsome, overly polite in that disturbing foreigner's way. He had a sad haircut and thick black-rimmed glasses. He was not of Ethel's race. She smiled and shook her head and said she was sorry. She was showing Kampon the door when Jimmy walked into the bar. He was probably on his way to find me. We have at least one good chat a day about the meaning of life, usually around that hour—about four in the afternoon, the happiest point in the daily curve of Jimmy's relationship to whiskey. But he ran into Kampon first and snatched him away from Ethel.

In his office Jimmy poured two drinks and sat the young engineer across from him at his desk. He told Kampon of his lifelong fascination with Kampon's part of the planet. "As the years go by," Jimmy said, "I think I'm becoming more and more of an Eastern mystic myself." He swept his arm in a gesture meant to encompass the entire world. "The physical plane means less and less to me every day."

"I am good worker," Kampon said.

"Of course you are," Jimmy said. "You come from an

industrious people. Not like us," he said, laughing and slapping himself in the stomach. "Lazy and fat." He leaned
over his desk. "Your people will inherit the earth. We will
be your servants."

Kampon was bewildered. He said nothing, but slid forward in his chair, his face hovering at the edge of Jimmy's
desk as if to inhale any life-giving vapors that might ema-
nate from the big American.

"I will teach you to wait on tables," Jimmy said. "You
will make tips—a custom we have. To Insure Prompt Service. You'll see." He shook Kampon's hand and smiled. The
teeth in Jimmy's smile are straight and fine and white in
front, and then, going back on either side, you see generous
helpings of gold.

His mouth is like another man's purse, is the rough English equivalent of what Kampon thought then in his native
tongue.

Jimmy led his new employee out the back door onto the
stretch of asphalt where the trucks back in to make deliv-
eries and empty the dumpsters. They strolled together
around the building into the parking lot. "This is a great
country," Jimmy said to Kampon, "even though our civilization is a tiny infant compared with yours."

"Very great country," Kampon said, nodding his head up
and down.

"Many types of people are needed to make a world,"
Jimmy said. "We don't have to destroy each other."

"Not destroy!" said Kampon, shaking his head and
hands with alarm. He stopped alongside his red Mustang.
Inside the car were four other young men from Thailand,

attending college in America. "My friends," Kampon explained, smiling and pointing to them.

Four clear-complected faces looked out at Jimmy, each one framed by a helmet of lustrous black hair. Jimmy called them out of the car to look them over. *All right,* he thought, *I see what I have to do.* After he had hired them all, Jimmy discovered that the Thai students were forbidden to hold jobs in the United States under the terms of their student visas. This in itself was not a disaster. Keeping people off the books is as common as bread in the restaurant business. But then Jimmy learned that they had no money and nowhere to live. They'd been put out of their college dormitory that very morning.

This was how Jimmy explained it to Victor: the Thai students would live in the carriage house only for the summer, three or four months, the restaurant's busiest season. And the trees and rampant vegetation around the carriage house make it a dark, unpleasant place in the summer anyway. Then, the instant they went back to school in September, a work crew would transform the place and Victor's family would dwell there in time for the fall foliage.

And this was how Victor responded to Jimmy's explanation: a chocolate ricotta pie pitched against the metal door of the walk-in cooler he uses to store his decadent desserts. We've lived with Victor for almost a month since then— his psyche collapsing darkly like a dying star—amid eruptions of tantrums, insults, and erratic pastry production. And now, attempted murder.

.   .   .

I pull into the long tree-lined drive that leads down to the sprawling white form of Inn Essence nestled in a shady grove on a defunct spur of the Erie-Lackawanna line. Twenty years ago, when Jimmy opened this place, the train was still running on this stretch of track—stopping at the old rambling inn this actually once was—and the land out there on the interstate where you see all those Martian-looking mirror-faced corporate headquarters was nothing but pasture full of cow plops. Now our parking lot can hold more than two hundred cars, though only a handful are in it so far today.

I park all the way down at the end, near the woods behind the dumpsters. As soon as I set foot on the shaded path to the carriage house, Bucky comes running out the door to meet me. He's the sweet little guy of the Thai group, gregarious and completely devoid of guile. Just like Victor to pick on the littlest one. Maybe I should forget about peace, I think, and help the Thai students finish Victor off.

"Hello, Señor Buck," I say when he reaches me on the path. "I hear you had a little run-in with Mr. Cream Puff."

"I get kill almost!" he says, grabbing my arm and imploring me with his wonderful almond eyes. Then he releases my arm and steps back and makes the motions of a big knife piercing his chest. He falls to one knee with this great blade inside him, his protruding teeth making it all the more heartbreaking. "Almost!" he cries.

"Why did he come after you, Buck?"

"I do no thing!" he says.

"Nothing?" I say. "You didn't eat any of his goodies?"

"No!"

"You didn't laugh at him? Snicker when his back was turned?"

"Snicker?"

I demonstrate a snicker for Bucky, hand over my mouth. "No!"

"OK, I believe you." I pat his back and help him stand up.

"Bad man!" he says with a shudder. "Very terrorful!"

"Calm down, Buck," I say. "We'll fix it up."

"Thank!" he says, and we walk together up the path.

"Bucky" is not Bucky's actual name. The waitresses named him Bucky because of his teeth. He doesn't understand that, fortunately, and he likes the name. In fact, all the Thai students are quite pleased with the nicknames they were given by the waitresses almost immediately upon their arrival; it makes them feel very American. Plus, they're much bigger flirts than even the waitresses are, and receiving any nickname at all from a woman signifies something pretty good in their book.

We step into the carriage house. It's dark inside even though the luminescent orange polyester curtains are open. What little light comes through the windows is soaked up instantly by wall paneling so depressingly cheap that the wood-grain pattern repeats exactly every eighteen inches. Rocky and Toots are sitting on the ratty sofa in the living room, decked out in the black satin-lapeled toreador jackets that Jimmy has his waiters and busboys wear. But they have their clip-on bow ties in their breast pockets and they're showing no signs of going in to start the lunch shift. Kampy and Buzz, off until dinner anyway, are sunk cross-legged in armchairs. The house is full of bad vibrations, a humid, conspiratorial air. "Hi, dudes," I say.

Nobody says anything. Kampy, my best buddy among the Thai workers, stares at me with a wistful face.

"Look, guys," I say. "Here's the thing about Victor. Victor is a sick man. He has visions. He sees things that aren't there. He hears voices. That's why he was in the hospital before you started working here."

"So why Mister C take him from hospital to here?" Rocky says. "Why not stay at hospital if sick?"

"It's not that simple, Rocky. The hospital is very expensive in America, and Victor is not crazy enough to stay there all the time anyway. Plus, his desserts are famous. And he wasn't always crazy. He lost his mind while he was working here. Many years of service. Mister C feels responsible. You understand that, don't you? Isn't that the way it would be in your country? Wouldn't a boss feel responsible for a sick worker?"

"But not responsible for Thai students," Toots says.

"Yes, responsible for you too. He gave you this house to live in, didn't he? He likes you. That's what caused the problem. Victor is jealous. His feelings are hurt."

"What about Thai worker feelings?" Buzz says.

"Yes, what about?" Rocky says, shaking the straight black luster of his hair.

Next to him on the sofa, Toots holds up an arm and grabs the flesh of it with his other hand. "What about Thai worker skin?" he says, shaking his forearm and grimacing.

So things are much worse here than I thought. And meantime, Kampy is just sitting there letting me dangle in the breeze. "Kamp," I say. "You understand, right? You appreciate this difficult situation."

"What I can say?" Kampy says. "Bloodfall happening at this place."

"No," I say, "that's not true. None happened, and none is going to happen." I turn to Rocky and Toots on the sofa. "Come on, you guys. Take Bucky inside and have some lunch. And then I want you to get out there and throw some food at those customers like only you know how."

"Very bad man," they say, but grudgingly they clip on their bow ties.

"Kampy," I say, "let's take a little walk."

He gets up and follows me outside. In the sunlight he looks me up and down as if seeing me for the first time. I'm wearing my pink Converse high-tops, wiped-out blue jeans, and a T-shirt with a cartoon of some happy snow peas dancing above the slogan BE A HUMAN BEAN.

I'm the salad man here at Inn Essence.

Kampy meditates on my T-shirt for a minute, moving the words around in his mouth. Finally he shakes his head and lets it go.

I put my hand on his shoulder and lead him along the path, which is dappled by flashes of yellow light coming down through the trees. We emerge from the cool, shady grove, and then we stroll along the edge of the underbrush that covers the old railroad tracks. Grasshoppers are springing out of the dandelions like trick party favors; the air is full of spicy weed-smells. It's a beautiful June. On either side of the abandoned tracks, thick stands of trashy sumac trees have grown to a height of forty feet or so and then fanned out flat on top into a canopy of pointy finger leaves. They give the back of the restaurant a jungle feeling.

I point up at the sinewy, sour-smelling trees. "Does Thailand look like this, Kamp? These kinds of trees? Little hills like that in the distance?"

Kampy looks up at the sumacs and then all around himself. He half shakes, half nods his head. "Maybe someway," he says. "Yes, little bit."

I laugh. "The sky is blue over there?"

He laughs too. "Yes, sky is blue."

We sit down on a fallen tree next to the railroad bed.

"Yes, we have railroad in Thailand," Kampy says, not waiting for me to ask. "Very similar."

"Hey, Kamp," I say. "Mister C had another brainstorm. He thinks I should have you teach me to speak Thai. So I can become more of a citizen of the world. He was telling me the other day."

Kampy smiles. "Very hard for you," he says. "Not like English."

"But I know you're a good teacher. I've been hearing about these cooking lessons of yours."

Here Kampy laughs out loud. "Oh-ho," he says. "Mister C say, 'Kampon, I must know true Thai way of cooking. Tell me exact way you eat in your house over there. Maybe I serve some of these things here at restaurant.' I tell him, 'American people not like Thai homestyle, Mister C.' But he not listen."

"Yes, he's good at that."

"He say, 'Kampon, food is key to world culture. All people must learn to eat together.' "

"Sounds like our boss, all right."

"But is not true."

"No?"

"People are different ways in this world, Jeffrey. People have loyalness with their own way. I, Kampon, understand this. Victor scream and bang at Thai workers. Mister C say no thing to Victor. Now Victor do violence against Bucky. You, Jeffrey, my friend, yes, but you say, 'Kampon, have forgetfulness.' No, Jeffrey. Thai workers must glue their selves in one lump."

"I agree with that, Kampy. I think you should stick together. But look. Jimmy will get Victor to go back on his medicine, and then everything will be fine."

"No, Jeffrey. Not true. Thai people can never work here tomorrow again, unless."

"Unless what?"

"Mister C must punish Victor." He stands up and walks away from me, out to the parking lot, "Farewell," he says, holding up his hand.

I stand up too. "Kampy, I'm going to see you in a few hours," I say. "When you come on for dinner."

"My heart flows," Kampy says, his hand on his breast. Then he cocks his head quizzically and stares at me, and suddenly he starts to laugh. "Oh, human bean," he says. "I got you. That's a funny one."

I scuffle back through the underbrush toward the restaurant, passing by the *Aqua Marie* on the way. This is Jimmy's cabin cruiser, a thirty-two-foot monster he keeps parked on its trailer in a clearing next to the dumpsters. The boat is named in honor of Jimmy's wife—the Invisible

Woman, we call her. I've heard Marie Constanopoulos's voice on the phone but I've never seen her; except for Manny, who's been here forever, no one at Inn Essence has ever met the woman our boss is married to. Part of Jimmy's arrangement with Marie is that she has nothing to do with the restaurant and is expected never to come here for any reason. Other aspects of Marie's conjugal life are speculated upon endlessly by the waitresses, who get what they can out of Manny and invent the rest. Marie is commonly presumed to have an unbelievable wardrobe, unlimited money to spend, and at least one handsome lover, if not a brace of handsome lovers—nice young ones in their twenties, the waitresses say, if she's got any brains. Even a nineteen-year-old wouldn't be out of the question; any woman can stand to recharge occasionally with a nineteen-year-old, the waitresses tell me.

The waitresses think that Marie Constanopoulos's situation comes as close to perfection as anything women have achieved in the history of the world.

But, even more than Marie, the waitresses have to wonder about Ethel, our hostess here at Inn Essence. How has she hung on all this time? Why does she put up with Jimmy's crap? What is she getting? What lies is he telling her? What does she feel when she answers the phone and hears Jimmy's wife on the other end? What goes through poor Ethel's mind when she walks out back and sees a huge fine cabin cruiser with the wife's name painted on it in letters two feet high?

I understand the waitresses' fascination, but I think they might as well be doing algebra with angels or trying to see the human soul by sprinkling cornstarch on people as they die. Me, I have an old friend in California named Ricky, a psychologist. Ricky has the word on this. "Nobody understands the boy-girl stuff, Jeffrey," Ricky says. "Not even God."

I walk across the loading area to the outside door of Jimmy's office, which is actually a one-bedroom apartment in its own small wing at the back of the restaurant. This is where for three years now Jimmy has been making love to Ethel. The blinds on the office windows are shut today, but behind the closed screen door the wooden door is ajar. I rap on the aluminum frame and call through the screen. "Bwana Jim, the natives are restless. I think you may have a revolt on your hands here. Spears and arrows may start flying out of the trees any minute now."

He doesn't answer me. When I cross the threshold, I smell Ethel's strong perfume. The waitresses say she alternates between Opium and Poison. If somebody comes out with a perfume called Sex or Death, straight out, Ethel will wear it. But then, so will everybody else. The woman herself is on the sofa, with a Scotch sour in one hand and a handkerchief in the other. She's had her hair done since yesterday, tinted a light bronze this time and sprayed into stiff swirls around her head. She's wearing a white silk blouse and a baby-blue suit. Her eyes are red and she's dabbing at her nose with the hanky. The bottle of Dewar's is on the coffee table—one third gone and it's not even noontime. Between Jimmy and Ethel, they're killing a good liter of it a day.

"Trouble in Thailand?" she says, tilting her head toward the carriage house.

"Well, Victor tried to murder Bucky this morning and they're a little upset about it, that's all."

"I know, I heard," Ethel says. She takes a long drag on her cigarette and then sips her drink, smoke pouring out of her face over the glass. She puts her stockinged feet up on the coffee table. "They'll get over it."

"I don't think so, Ethel. This was pretty abusive, even for Victor."

"Honey, we all have to take our share of abuse, now don't we?"

"Some of us have to take more than others."

"Tell me about it," she says. "Actually, I thought it was kind of amusing, Victor running around the parking lot in those little Italian shoes, waving that big knife. We don't have enough excitement around here."

Ethel has her own waitress-given nickname. "Miss Frosty," they call her.

"Jimmy around?" I say.

"No, he's out looking for the mad muffin." Her own joke makes her smile. "The king of pork loin is searching for the mad muffin."

"That's pretty good."

"It really is, isn't it? I'm pretty creative, aren't I? I don't give myself enough credit."

"Most people don't."

"Some people give themselves too much," she says.

"The Thai students want Jimmy to punish Victor," I say.

"Ha," Ethel says.

"They say Jimmy must make some show of righting this wrong. Their heritage demands it."

Ethel leans her head back and cackles at the ceiling, coughing on her drink. "I didn't think anybody could do it today," she says, "but you're doing it. You're making me laugh." She giggles in a macabre way for a half minute or so until, with no perceptible transition, she's weeping.

"Ethel, is something wrong?"

We all have to pretend that we don't know about Ethel's life, how her husband left her on account of Jimmy and how she's been waiting two years now for Jimmy to do the right thing.

"None of your business," she says through the handkerchief. After a minute she gets herself under control, blots her eyes, and has another taste of her drink. "What exactly do they want Jimmy to do to Victor, by the way?"

"I don't know," I say. "A gesture. Something to restore their dignity. Make him apologize, I suppose."

"Can you imagine Victor apologizing to anybody about anything?"

"No."

"Me neither. Maybe you and Jimmy can philosophize about it when he gets back. Maybe he'll have a theory about it. He was looking for you before. He wanted to ask you about a word. It's on his desk."

I walk over to Jimmy's desk. There's a legal pad with the word *epistemology* written on it, spelled incorrectly.

Ethel says, "He wanted to know if that word meant there were some things he'd never get to the bottom of."

I think about it for a minute. "Yeah, I guess you could say that."

.   .   .

Nine months ago I started here busing tables. Then, after a couple of weeks, Jimmy gave me my choice of moving up to waiter or going to the kitchen. Most people would have chosen to be a waiter, for the tips. I didn't think I needed daily contact with the public, and I certainly didn't need to work under Ethel out there. But there was another reason I chose the kitchen, one that surprised me as much as anyone else. After two weeks of observing the impeccable ballet of our chefs and tasting the results, I discovered that I wanted to be able to cook like that.

So they brought me back and started me in on salads. At most restaurants this would have been like permanent exile; salad chefs are usually a notch above busboys and going nowhere. But at Inn Essence people have respect for salad. I'm a colleague here, encouraged to be creative. And I'm in training for bigger things.

Ordinarily I show up in the kitchen in the middle of the afternoon and scrub my vegetables. I wash my lettuce, reserving the best leaves for cups and baskets, tearing the rest into pieces. Then I get out my gleaming little knife for the magical part—the radish roses, the kiwi-fruit lotus pads, the celery palm trees, the gift bows out of cantaloupe shavings, the apples peeled and carved into carnations, the whole vegetable fantasy world I've learned to do so well.

But now, early in the dinner hour, all my salad chores are done and I'm having my latest cooking lesson. I'm learning to make the famous stuffed medallions of veal, as done by the Venezuelan-born Manny Quintero, the head chef of Inn Essence. We're together at his counter, our backs to the ovens, cutting the veal and talking about the stuffing of legend.

So far I've heard nothing from Jimmy. If he's lost interest in where things stand with the Thai students, that's his lookout.

"I use butter," Manny says. "You hear? Butter. I use fresh garlic, fresh mushrooms, only fresh herbs. Some so-called chefs, they use soybean oil, garlic and mushrooms from bottles, herbs from little cans." He tosses a veal medallion on the pile and wipes his hands on his long cook's apron. "I pity the bastards."

"Me too," I say, nodding my head.

Manny's two assistant chefs are working to our left, at the range, in a flurry of smoke and steam, putting up orders for the dining room. Rocky and Toots arrive to load the plates onto their trays. They're aloof and businesslike, still full of fear and hurt pride.

"Are the citizens of America happy tonight?" I ask them. "Do they have that hungry light in their eyes? Men, are they ripping those salads apart?"

"Citizens pretty happy," says Toots.

Manny says, "When I cook, I like to think of them as people who stayed in this inn when they were young, and now, tonight, they're back for the first time in twenty years. It inspires me."

I take a step backward to look at him. "You're getting as dreamy as the guy who owns this place," I say. "And all this time I thought you were secretly driving the bus."

"I thought you were," he says.

Suddenly a high-pitched burst of Thai exclamation comes out of Rocky. He's staring at the back door of the restaurant, around the corner from Manny's ovens. Victor has just strolled in, dressed in his dazzling whites, right up to the towering puff of chef's toque. He must drive his car in this outfit. His feet are as tiny as a girl's in their little black pumps.

"What do you know," Manny calls out. "It's the mousse man. Hey, mousse man, we don't have any desserts tonight. What happened, Mister Mousse?"

Victor ignores Manny. Instead, he looks at me. "Will you get a load of this," he says, pulling the big metal handle of his walk-in to open it. "Manny is training Jimmy's little pet."

He waits for me to respond but I don't give him the satisfaction. He steps into his walk-in, and the door snaps shut behind him. Rocky and Toots are simmering in the hot red light of the warming lamps, looking mean. "Waiters," I say to them, "pick up your orders and take them out to the people. Be professionals."

They do so, but their concern is justified. There's something very eerie about seeing Victor in the kitchen at this hour of the day. His routine is to start in the early morning and be long gone by the time the first blackened red snapper comes off the grill at night. I refuse to believe he's here out of guilt over leaving us without desserts.

"We have to send that boy back to the nut bin," I say to Manny.

"No, they can't help him there," Manny says, shaking his head. "They just give him drugs and stare at him all day, make him worse than he was before. He's happy when he bakes. So I say let him bake. And when the man gets crazy, knock him down."

I look at Manny flexing his nut-brown arm. He's referring to the way he handled the episode last March. Victor comes out of his walk-in and installs himself in the L-shaped baking zone at the rear of the kitchen, where he has his long counters of work space, his own special ovens and range. He doesn't look tranquilized to me. He's removed several big aluminum trays of flaky pastry puffs from his cooler, and now he sticks them in their sides with the business end of a pastry bag, squirting them full of chocolate-cream filling. He seems to be taking unusual delight in this operation.

I hear Ethel call my name. She's standing inside the kitchen's swinging doors. "Jimmy wants to see you," she says, nodding in the direction of his office. I see her take note of Victor's presence. Then she shoulders open the right-hand door and spins away through it.

"Boss wants to see his little pet," Manny says to me, really enjoying himself, showing all of his gleaming tusks.

"Give me a break, Manny," I say.

"One break coming up," he says.

I walk out from behind the chef's area, untying my apron on the way. I stop at the swinging doors and look through their windows. Ethel is at the waiters' station, talking to Kampy, Buzz, and Bucky. They're gesturing with their hands and she's nodding her head. Rocky and Toots appear with their empty table trays and join in this conversation. Ethel is actually listening to them, which is odd; she's not known for her sympathy, certainly not to the Thai students, whom she's tried to ignore from the day they started.

Two waitresses, Cheryl and Nadine, are sitting here in the kitchen by the uniform closet, having a cigarette. I mention what I'm seeing out there—Ethel being chummy with the Thai waiters.

"Oh, yeah, she's the good mother tonight," Cheryl says, nodding her head so that the plumes of smoke from her nostrils make waves. "She had a big fight with Jimmy, and now she's being real nice to everybody."

"They should fight all the time," Nadine adds. "It makes her almost like a person."

A smoke ring leaves Cheryl's mouth. "They do fight all the time."

Stepping out of the kitchen, I nod to Ethel and the guys. I walk into the open corridor with the rest rooms and pay phones, turning to take another look at them from the quiet carpeted dimness. Sometimes, in the middle of the dinner rush, Jimmy will stand here like this, next to the cigarette machines, watching the Thai waiters interact with the public and one another. He has an anthropologist's fascination with them as they make their way through the world; their customs and doings are deep, mysterious things to him.

His office door is all the way down at the end of the hall. I knock on it.

"Oh, it's you," he says when I walk in. "So what's going on out there? Do I still have a restaurant?" He's sitting slumped on the sofa, a heavy man in a gray tropical suit, shirt collar open, no tie, holding a Scotch-and-water in his lap.

"No man ever knows what he really has," I say.

He laughs with great Greek delight, eyes wrinkling,

golden teeth flashing in the corners of his mouth. "I like you, Jeffrey," he says. "I can always count on you." He points to a chair and I sit down. "You think it's easy being the guy in charge?"

"Of course not," I say. "It's hell."

"Correct." He sips his Scotch. The liter of Dewar's is still on the coffee table, maybe one drink left in it now. "Have I ever told you about when I was in Korea?"

"You've mentioned it."

"You wouldn't even have been born yet."

"No."

"I was a sergeant, did you know that?"

"You told me."

"It was an amazing thing, Jeffrey. Koreans were all around us. Everywhere you looked you saw Korean people and Korean life."

"Well, Jimmy, you were in Korea."

"Exactly. I'm saying it was their country, but we were there. We were the strangers."

"I'm with you so far."

"But the weird thing was, Jeffrey, *we were in charge.* We were there to solve their problem. They were looking to us for *answers.* And Jeffrey?"

"Yeah?"

"We didn't even know what the question was. We didn't know the first thing about those people's lives. I was giving out orders, for Christ's sake, and I didn't even know what I was doing over there. But for the first time in my life I had incredible power. And I discovered something."

"What?"

"I loved it. I loved the power. It didn't matter at all that

I was an ignorant schmuck. Having that power canceled out everything else."

"Strange. Listen, Jimmy, Victor's here. He's baking in the kitchen right now."

"Yeah, I know, I just talked to him." He parts the blinds on the window next to the sofa and looks out at the carriage house. Often he secretly observes the comings and goings of the Thai students from this window. "I learned another thing in the service," he says. "You always hear that people everywhere are basically the same, that all anybody really wants is to be loved. That's true, but they also want to make sure nobody gets any but them."

"Jimmy, I think a lot of those people in Korea just wanted not to get shot by you or have a bomb dropped on their house. They wanted to wake up the next day, and that was about it."

"Those are the accidents of history, Jeffrey. I'm talking about the big, eternal things, like the fact that all people are greedy and self-centered and they make excuses for it with ideas like 'honor' and 'saving face.'"

"You talked to Ethel about the Thai students."

He shakes his head and deeply sighs her name. "Ethel." Then he belts down the rest of his drink. "What am I going to do about Ethel?"

"She was crying in here before."

"She cries all the time," he says. "OK, everybody wants a piece of Jimmy. All right, fine, I accept that. But Ethel's not satisfied with her piece, and she's letting it ruin her life. Let me tell you something, Jeffrey. I never promise anybody anything I can't deliver. If I can't deliver, I don't promise. It's a good rule, one you could live by if you're

interested. Ethel has gotten everything she was ever promised and a lot more. If she wants to walk out, she can walk
out."

"Is that what she wants to do? Walk out?"

"No, I told you. She wants to be the only puppy in the
litter. Since she can't have that, she's going to find a different way to make me miserable every day. But tonight she's
unbelievable. Tonight—get this—she wants me to punish
Victor for running after Bucky with the knife."

"No kidding."

"Yeah, she insists on it. The dignity of her staff requires
it, she says. I said forget it. I'm not punishing anybody."

"Maybe you should. If it would keep her happy."

"Jeffrey, yesterday Ethel couldn't stand the Thai people,
all right? Don't argue with me, I know how to handle this.
Now listen carefully, kid, you're about to learn something.
Here's what I do. I call the Thai students in and—humbly,
with gratitude for good service—I offer them more money.
Right out of the blue, I give them a big raise."

"I'm sure they'll appreciate that."

"But I say nothing to them about Victor. Victor's name
is never mentioned. I make no connection between Victor
and their reward. OK? And now, do I then turn around and
punish Victor? Far from it. Pay attention, Jeffrey, I've
never let anyone else in on this. *I call Victor in and I give
him more money too.* In fact, I've already done it. You see
what I'm saying? Money is love, Jeffrey, and now everybody
has more than they had before. Presto, peace is restored to
the garden. All the animals can live happily together again.
But the brilliant part is that this love doesn't make judg-
ments. It doesn't take sides. It's love that forgives. Frankly,

Jeffrey, it's the love Jesus was talking about. I resolve the conflict by giving everybody more money, Victor and the Thai students equally, even though Victor did something very bad."

"He tried to kill Bucky."

"Oh, no, something much worse than that. Something to hurt me personally, his benefactor and friend."

"He did? What?"

"He called Immigration, the jerk."

"He didn't."

"Oh, yes, he did. He ratted on me about the Thai students. He admitted it to me here in this office just now. He called them from his house, and then he came back here to be on hand for the excitement. He strolled in and sat right there, puffed up with his secret betrayal. But he couldn't carry it off. He became remorseful and confessed. I let him stew in his own guilt for a minute, and then I just blew him away with his raise. You think he was confused before? Now he's really confused. But he's confused by love, which is good."

"Jimmy, what about Immigration?"

"Yeah, them. You're right, we should take some defensive action. We should hide the Thai students. Would you do that for me? Go hide the boys and then buzz me when the feds get here."

I'm up out of my chair and walking away when something occurs to me. "This idea of putting love in people's paychecks—you ever try that on Ethel?"

"Are you kidding? Ethel makes so much money here now it's ridiculous. But that doesn't work for her anymore. It's my fault. I let Ethel get keyed in to a different symbol.

You know, I always wondered why mystics and saints denied the body; why priests, those poor bastards, had to be celibate. Now I think I get it. Jesus kept the company of whores, but I've never read anything about him messing around with them. Sex changes everything, Jeffrey, don't ask me why."

I tell Jimmy my friend Ricky's line about boy-girl business.

"A friend of yours said that?" Jimmy says. "Hey, does this guy want a job? The man who said that can come work for me anytime."

"I'll let him know," I say. "Now I better get out there and save our butts."

"Good. You do that."

I'm halfway out the door when he calls me back again.

"Hey, one second," he says. "I had a few recipe ideas I wanted to run by you. Wait till you hear these. What would you think of moussaka with—brace yourself—hot curry and a peanut sauce? Or feta-cheese pie with ginger and snow peas? And how does baklava with coconut milk and litchi nuts grab you?"

"Don't tell me," I say. "Greek-Thai cuisine."

"You got it," he says. "Inspired, right? A whole new contribution. East meets West. Two ancient cultures united. I hope Manny doesn't give me a hard time about it. You get to be my age, Jeffrey, you start thinking about the big picture. You start asking some basic questions about your existence. 'Did his menu reflect his vision of life? Did he *have* a vision of life? Did he have anything new to offer? Did he have anything to say?' Things like that."

.   .   .

I hurry out to the head of the corridor and stand behind
the cigarette machines, scanning the dining room. Just inside the front door, next to the sign that says OUR HOSTESS
WILL SEAT YOU, are two hard guys in rumpled suits. They
look hungry, all right, but not for anything we serve here.
They're swiveling their heads on their big necks, checking
the place out real good. Our hostess will seat you! For the
first time in my career at Inn Essence I'd give anything to
see Ethel walk around the corner—her face carved out of
flesh-colored ice, her hair sprayed into a bronze battle helmet. She could make crème brûlée out of these guys. But,
incredibly, in the middle of the dinner rush, she's not on
duty. Just across from me, Nadine is picking up a drink
order at the end of the bar. I sidle up to her and point out
the feds. "Head those guys off, Nadine!" I whisper. "Stall
'em. They're here to bust us for illegal aliens." She looks
back and forth between me and the front door like I've just
dropped down from Neptune.

"Do it, Nadine!" I cry. Then I burst through the swinging doors into the kitchen. The Thai waiters are nowhere
to be seen. Neither is Victor. But then I see that all the
way at the back of the kitchen, by the exit to the parking
lot, the door of Victor's walk-in is just closing.

Manny, still doing the veal medallions, sees me standing
there. "Here's how they look when you're done," he calls
out, holding on his palm the glistening meat wrapped
neatly around its stuffing.

I run up to the glass partition beneath the warming

lamps. "Never mind the veal, Manny!" I bark at him. "Where are the Thai students?"

He looks around. "I don't know," he says. "They were just here."

"Manny, Victor called Immigration! They're at the front door!"

He catches this hot potato like the pro he is, dropping the veal and bolting out of his work space toward the dining room. I run the other way past him and around the corner to Victor's walk-in. I'm going to take care of Victor, I think to myself. I'm going to fix this clown. I yank open the door of his cooler and leap inside.

In doing so, I smack into Ethel and nearly knock her down.

"What the hell are you doing in here?" I snap at her. She snaps the same thing at me. Then the door of the walk-in snaps shut and I can't see anything. The only light in Victor's huge cooler comes from two low-wattage bare bulbs on either side of the ceiling fan, and my eyes are accustomed to the brightness outside. It's cold, but deliciously so, compared to the swelter of the kitchen.

I'm about to tell Ethel what I'm doing in here when my eyes adjust enough to see that all the Thai workers are in here with her. I throw my arms around her shoulders. "You're beautiful, Ethel!" I say. "Good going! But is it safe enough?"

She pushes me away. "Safe enough for what?" she says with great irritation.

And then I see Victor. He's sitting against the rear wall of the walk-in, legs stretched out in front of him, arms behind his back, his hands and feet bound with crisp cloth napkins fresh from the linen service. His mouth is wide open as if in amazement, but that's because one of his own cream puffs has been stuffed all the way into it to gag him. His narrowed eyes are fixed on me—not with fear or rage or even supplication, not with any emotion at all, but with the unnerving vacancy of a man in shock. I look at him more closely in the thin yellow light. Squiggles of dark brown chocolate cream are all over his body—stripes of it up and down his arms and legs and outlining the pockets and buttons of his baker's uniform. He looks like a gingerbread man in reverse, brown frosting on white. Bucky is kneeling on the floor next to him, the chocolate-cream-filled pastry bag in his hands.

"Do his face now, Bucky," Ethel says. "He needs some nice eyebrows, doesn't he, boys?"

All the Thai students giggle their agreement. Bucky chortles with delight and sets to work on the brows, squeezing thick lines of chocolate onto Victor's face. Suddenly Victor comes to life and struggles violently for a moment, making scary animal noises around the cream puff in his mouth and messing up the frosting on his eyebrows.

"Baking man not want to be cookie," Bucky says, flashing all his protruding teeth. He puts some chocolate on Victor's nose, and then he sets to work decorating Victor's tall white hat. Kampy and Toots and Rocky and Buzz are all smiling and nodding their heads up and down. Then Kampy turns to me.

"Mister C understand Thai worker feelings," he says. "He send Miss Ethel to tell us good idea of punishment for Victor. We have such ways like this in Thailand too. No person get hurt, and Thai workers have honor restored. Mister C is very wise man. America is fair country."

I look at Ethel. She glares at me. I turn to the metal door of the walk-in and press my ear against it. The bitter chill gives me a headache instantly, but I stay there.

"We have a report that you have employed illegal alien workers from Thailand," I hear Immigration saying, faintly through the door. *"Let's go, chef. Where are they? Let's see these Thai workers."*

Victor sees me listening at the door and he starts making a fuss again in the back of the cooler, bucking and snorting some guttural sounds. But his walk-in was once the inn's meat locker, with solid walls and a heavy rubber seal around the opening; no one will ever hear him out there.

I put my ear back to the cold agony of the door. Manny's distant voice materializes, the volume fluctuating up and down. He must be following Immigration around the kitchen. *"Thailand?"* he says. *"You mean Venezuela? It's me you looking for? Manny Quintero from Venezuela? But I ain't no illegal, man! I got my papers twenty years now! Just 'cause I'm a foreigner one time you come after me? Let's go to my house, I show you some papers. Gonna be egg on you faces, misters."*

Ethel slides a tray of Victor's cream puffs halfway out of a rack, picks one up, and raises it above her head. She throws like a girl, but her aim is good. Chocolate cream and flaky pastry splatter across Victor's face. The Thai students applaud. Then Bucky stands up and Ethel passes cream puffs out to the boys. They all get one and wait for me to get mine.

Now Jimmy comes storming into the kitchen. *"Where*

did you get this crap?" he says. *"Who said these things about me? Where is my accuser? Let him show his face. Come out wherever you're hiding, you bastard."*

"It was an anonymous tip," Immigration says. "On the telephone. We don't know who it was."

"Come on, Jeffrey, take your cream puff," Ethel says.

"You don't know who it was?" Jimmy screams. *"You don't know who it was? Well, I know who it was! I'll tell you who it was! It was the man in the moon! You come to my place of business with this slander, this libel, these filthy lies, trying to get my name in the papers, trying to ruin my good reputation, trying to shut down the nicest restaurant in New Jersey on the basis of a telephone prank? I could make a stink about this you wouldn't believe! I know people in Trenton! I could have your jobs! I could get you Border Patrol in the Texas scrub! For life! Get the hell out of my restaurant!"*

"I don't want one," I say.

"I knew it," Ethel says. "Sensitive Jeffrey doesn't want a cream puff. That's because you are a cream puff, Jeffrey. This is a ritual; everybody has to do it. Take it."

I remove my ear from the door. "No, Ethel."

Now the Thai students are confused. Jeffrey's not taking a cream puff. They stand there looking at me, not knowing what to do.

"Fine, Jeffrey. You don't have to participate. But you don't get to stay and watch the fun, either. Just open the door and get out."

"No," I say. "I can't do that."

"Oh, you are such a wimp, Jeffrey. You are such a little teacher's pet. Never mind him," Ethel says to the Thai students. "This is the ancient American way. Mister C knows it, I know it. You have your old customs in Thailand, we have ours here. Throw those cream puffs, boys. Jeffrey's just anti-American, aren't you, Jeffrey?"

Pressing my head against the freezing metal door must have numbed my brain, because suddenly I'm dizzy and can't even talk to Ethel anymore. I have to close my eyes for a second to collect my thoughts. I have to see if I have this straight. I'm one of eight people hiding in a dim restaurant walk-in, our breath coming out of our faces in little mingling clouds. The proprietor of the walk-in is tied up on the floor, and federal agents are outside trying to bust us, but not for tying him up. The owner's mistress is calling me names because I won't take a cream puff she's offering me, while five young men from a distant land are looking at me with questioning eyes, the sweet pastries of revenge already in their hands. They're waiting for me to confirm that whatever we're doing is indeed the way justice is done in my country.

Can I deny it?

GOODYEAR

We're invited to a cookout this afternoon at Wendy and Bill's; they live in a trailer park in the country, on the other side of town. It's the wrong time of year for a cookout—I told Wendy so when she called last week to invite us. People don't have cookouts in November, I said, even in northern California. It's too cold. Wendy said she'd been having good feelings about the weather. The earth was sending warmth vibrations to her, she said. Since she called it's been ridiculously nice, getting warmer every day. Katy says that over on campus the kids have started going wild—running outside without their clothes, throwing water balloons, declaring classes canceled.

Now it's actually hot, even out here in the hills. Through the windshield the sky looks like a blue idea the earth is having. I wish we had a convertible, and I think convertibles are dangerous and silly. The squirrels are confused by the weather, chasing each other through the evergreens instead of foraging for nuts. Red-winged blackbirds are flying into and out of the woods and lining the guardrails on either side of the road. Probably they should have flown somewhere else by now—Miami, Buenos Aires.

We're taking a drive, trying to get in the mood for a cookout.

"Let's just forget about what's going to happen," Katy says. "Just for today, OK? We can fight about it tomorrow. It's too nice out today for fighting."

"I like that," I say. "The way I become the bad guy. We're not fighting."

"Whatever it is we're doing," she says.

The big dark disks of Katy's sunglasses give her a tough, inscrutable face. I can't tell anything by looking at her. I assume my sunglasses do the same for me. I check in the rearview mirror. They do—I look like a real bad guy.

Fletcher, Katy's dissertation director, has invited her to go to Florence with him in January. He's taking a group of undergraduates there for the spring semester and wants Katy to be his assistant. This is the same Fletcher I've been hearing about all year, the one who cannot confine himself to pretty graduate women but sleeps with even his freshman students. People in Katy's department joke about sending sympathy cards to Fletcher's wife. But I met her once at a party, and I think she's in on it. Maybe Fletcher takes pictures and brings them home. He's not bringing his wife to Florence.

I brooded for a week after hearing about this invitation. Finally I said, "The man's a satyr, an actual aberration.

You've said so yourself. He's asking you to be his concubine in Italy; it's as plain as day. I can't believe you're even considering it."

"I knew that was what was bothering you," she said. "More than just the separation from me."

"The separation is bothering me."

"But before Florence ever came up you couldn't stop thinking about the chance to work with Daryl and Eric in New York. Something was telling you not to pass that up. Now you can go. Some time away from each other would do us good, give us a chance to see how we feel."

"Let's be honest. Let's tell the truth. This is the end."

"I am telling the truth. I don't know what this is. I need to do my work. You want some truth about yourself?"

"No."

"I can't remember the last time I saw you happy. I've been looking at you, and you're not happy. Even when nothing at all was hanging over our heads you weren't happy. What do you want to be unhappy for?"

"I don't think I understand how you're using the word 'happy,' " I said.

"Now that you mention it, neither do I. I have no idea what I meant by that. Forget it."

Today Katy decided to go to Florence with Fletcher. He's a brilliant man, she says, full of professional clout, and she's not even slightly attracted to him. Fletcher won't be putting a finger on her, she says. Going to Florence will mean a different caliber of dissertation—something that could end up as a book—and real chances for a job. She wonders why she wasn't this ambitious to begin with, why she seems to have this tendency to wait around for things to happen to her. She feels better and stronger and more in control already. Not going to Florence would be just as crazy, Katy says, as my not grabbing the chance to go to New York and make a lot of money learning video.

Daryl and Eric have room for a new person on their crew. They've signed a big deal to make instructional tapes for an insurance company. It should take about six months and pay a lot of rent. When they're not paying the rent, Daryl and Eric do video for rock bands. I've seen their studio; it's full of astonishing technology—sublime, transcendental stuff. Everything in the place is on the computer. Everywhere you look, little red lights are flashing on and off as the machines remember things and make decisions. People are standing in line in New York hoping to work with that kind of equipment. Daryl and Eric are doing me a favor. It could turn into a career, they say, laughing over the phone when they call me late at night. A genteel, electronic life in media, just like theirs. What else am I doing?

The road has curved and climbed to the top of this hill; now it levels out up here in the sunlit trees. On the tape player, Derek and the Dominoes launch into "Why Does Love Got to Be So Sad?," one of my favorite songs since I first heard it, a long time ago. I turn the volume up. The lyrics are supposed to convey remorse and bewilderment, but the music itself says, Get up and dance your ass to the moon.

Katy turns the volume down. "You always play it too loud," she says. "It ruins it."

"You used to like to hear it loud," I say.

"Not as loud as you," she says.

I leave it turned down and drive along, thinking about the time we've spent together. I think of it as a year composed of a million individual moments of sympathy and joy, each of them wafting up and away from us like a bubble or a balloon. That's what I'm envisioning—the essence escaping from people's lives in millions of bubbles, some big, some small—when I come around a sharp bend in the road and see the great silver-gray behemoth hovering in the sky in front of us.

"The Goodyear blimp!" I say.

"Oh," Katy says, seeing it. "There it is. It's big."

"Big?" I say. *"Big?"*

"Very big," she says.

What a monster it is, flashing in the sun, filling up the space between two dappled hilltops. I haven't seen it in years, don't remember it as quite this unearthly. I drive up until we're perpendicular to it; then I pull over and we get out. It's like a skyscraper that fell down and floated away, or a rocket ship lying on its side in the air. You cringe and expect it to fall on you, and it's scary. If you dreamt this thing, you'd wake up.

"I knew it was coming," Katy says.

"You did?"

"I heard about it at school. They're televising the football game today."

"You didn't tell me. You never even mentioned it."

A light breeze blows into the meadow next to the road, and the blimp actually bobs to and fro up there. Something comes over me when I see it move. I start running back and forth along the pasture fence with my head thrown back, taking deep breaths as if to breathe the blimp in.

That tires me out and I lie down on my back, my arms open as if to embrace it. I can see Katy out of the corner of my eye, leaning against a fence post with a bemused expression on her face.

Then the blimp swings around and floats away. We follow it for a while in the car, thrilled each time it comes into view through the trees. Finally I can't spot it anymore. Seeing the blimp has made me feel good again—tiny and lifted up out of myself. Katy is tickled by how much I like it. She likes me better when I like things, she says.

On the highway coming down out of the hills, you get a wonderful view of Bill and Wendy's trailer park. From that perspective, it seems to have been inspired by the ruins of Mayan civilization—its deeply terraced knoll tapering pyramid-fashion up to a small mesa on top, with pink and turquoise and baby-blue rectangles perched on each plateau. I can imagine Rudy Beck, the developer and landlord, coming across pictures of Mayan ruins and getting the inspiration to do a trailer park based on them, but the resemblance is probably accidental. Rudy is a widower in his sixties. He lives alone on a small farm up in back of Tanglewood Terraces, his name for the trailer park. Wendy invites Rudy to all her cookouts and patio parties, and usually he shows up. He has a few drinks and tells bad jokes and pats all the women on the back to see if they're wearing brassieres. Everybody thinks he's a wonderful old guy.

Bill and Wendy live in a lime-green trailer at the very top of the park. Their rig is a relic of the days when a mobile home was a thing of enchantment. On the inside it has that optimistic forties look—solid-oak paneling, counter-tops that pop out of the walls, chrome trim on everything. On the outside, though, it's a shack. The neighbors are embarrassed and want Rudy to tow Bill and Wendy's house away, but where the rubber tires used to be there are concrete blocks and rusted wheel hubs. They bought it where it stands. Wendy filled the trailer hitch with dirt and planted geraniums in it.

She's out in front when we pull up, gathering kindling for the pit barbecue. Some of her long brown hair has gotten tangled in the twigs she's holding.

"Katy and Saint Francis!" she says, skipping over to hug and kiss us as we get out of the car, poking us in the chests with her kindling. She's wearing khaki shorts and a pink halter top, and she looks very nice.

"Hey, Wendy," I say. "Awfully warm out here for November, isn't it?"

"I know," she says, beaming. "I knew it would be."

"I hope you haven't abused your magical powers," I say. "Surely you wouldn't cast a spell on the weather."

She steps back and brandishes one of the larger twigs. "That wasn't nice," she says. Her eyes are narrowed down to slits.

"I was joking," I say.

Wendy has studied magic, and sometimes she casts spells for her friends—for the common cold, unrequited love, job interviews, things like that. She put a matchmaking spell on Katy and me back when she was trying to fix us up; she told us about it afterward. She's working one now for Katy's dissertation. But Wendy does only white magic. Changing the weather would be black magic, even changing it for the better.

"Let me tell you what happens to people who joke about magic," she says. "Little things start to go wrong in their lives. Then bigger things." She taps my cheek a few times with her twig and smiles. "But I told you what a great day it would be," she says. "You heard it here first, O ye of little faith."

"I always believed you," I say. "I think Katy had doubts, though."

"Wait one minute," Katy says. "It was the other way around. He was the Doubting Thomas. I was the believer."

"That sounds more like it," Wendy says.

She takes Katy's hand, and they wander off to gather more kindling. They haven't had a chance to see each other in a while. When they reach the edge of the clearing where the trailer park meets the trees, they squat down and break dead branches scattered in the underbrush. I can hear the sound of their voices, though not the words themselves. Wendy is trying on Katy's sunglasses and surveying the trailer-studded slope, but I feel her looking sideways at me. She's nodding her head and saying something and putting her arm around Katy's shoulders. Wendy is a natural confidante, born with the gift for it. People sense this and tell her all their secrets, and she simply absorbs them like one of those mystics who take on the bad karma of others.

Once, before she knew Bill and before I knew Katy, Wendy and I were lovers. It lasted about a month. I remember it now as a month of my telling Wendy all my problems, over and over—why I'd just dropped out of graduate school, why I didn't know what I wanted to do, why I couldn't stop doing destructive things. I can't recall Wendy ever confiding much about herself. I thought I was in love with her, and when she ended our affair I waited for the grief to hit me. But I'd emptied all my sorrow into Wendy. There wasn't enough left for a broken heart.

I take our groceries into the kitchen, and then I head out to the backyard to fix up Wendy's birdbath—a three-foot concrete oyster shell with two cherubs perched on its lip. The boy cherub is standing up, lost in thought or looking at the sheep in Rudy's hilltop pasture. The girl cherub is sitting on the other side of the oyster shell, gesturing with a chubby arm to the boy cherub, trying to get his attention. The birdbath has an electric pump inside it; when you fill it up with water and turn it on, the boy cherub urinates endlessly into the shell.

Wendy and Bill are bored by the birdbath and don't keep it up, so the first thing I do when I come over here is hose it out and get it going. It makes me happy to see the birds enjoying their bath, splashing and carrying on. If I have some stale bread or birdseed, I throw it around the oyster shell. Then I sit in a lounge chair and watch the birds eat it up, meditating on the great differences between our lives. Sometimes I whistle their own tunes back to them, and they hop around in circles trying to figure out where the strange bird is. Wendy and Bill call me Saint Francis of Assisi now; they won't call me by my real name anymore.

While I'm hosing bird droppings off the cherubs, I hear Bill working across the road in the shed he rents from Rudy. Bill is a dedicated person. With his hands and a few simple tools he can do amazing things. Everything he knows he taught himself. He never went to school for it. He can make guitars and wooden flutes and play quite well on them. Lately he's been earning a living with reproductions of antique furniture. His own furniture designs didn't sell very well. One of Bill's passions is science fiction—he's read just about every sci-fi novel ever written—and people around here aren't ready for tables and chairs from outer space.

I plug in the birdbath and walk over to his shed. Inside, he's hand-rubbing a walnut love seat. He wants to go to a shopping center to buy some extra beer.

"Will we be back in time for the football game?" I say. "What time do football games start? I had my heart set on it."

"Football game?" Bill says. He picks up a screwdriver and pretends to screw something into my head. "Something's happened to Saint Francis of Assisi. He wants to watch football. On television, no less. He must have been out by himself in the woods again, having one of those visions."

I tell Bill that I want to watch the football game to see the Goodyear blimp, not to see the football.

He spread his arms and looks up at the ceiling. "My faith in him is restored," he says.

In my car on the way to the store, Bill is trying to convey what it was like when the blimp appeared above his trailer park yesterday. It sailed in and hovered right over the pasture in back of the house, as if scrutinizing Rudy's sheep out there. It was cigar-shaped, Bill says, and silver, and there was a cabin on the bottom for the aliens.

"They come from a highly advanced civilization," he says.

Best of all, Bill has proof that the blimp exists. Wendy took pictures of it, two entire rolls of color slides. The shopping center we're driving to has the overnight photo-finishing place where she dropped the film. Bill says Wendy is talking about doing a whole series of oil paintings of the blimp, paintings with a kind of cargo-cult energy behind them, mythological energy.

"She really got bitten by the blimp bug," he says. "She's totally blimped."

"Katy knew it was coming and she never even mentioned it. I think she takes blimps for granted."

"Could be," Bill says. "Or maybe she just didn't think of it."

"She's going to Florence with her creepy teacher."

"She is doing that? Well, people do these things. She has work she has to do."

"She's leaving, Bill. Taking off."

"She's coming back."

"Not necessarily."

"Oh. Well."

"I'm taking the video thing in New York."

"Into the madness with Daryl and Eric." He takes the hand I'm not steering with and shakes it. "We'll miss you, lucky dog. But we'll survive, even if you won't. You sound like your eyes are being plucked out. Admit you're happy about getting out of here while she's gone."

"I'm happy."

"Admit you're excited and wish you were going tomorrow."

"I'm excited. I wish I were going tomorrow."

At the shopping center, the young bloods are racing their cars around the parking lot with the tops down, tape players screaming, girlfriends dangling over the sides. Bill and I divide the labor: I go to the liquor store, he goes to the photo place.

The liquor store is really a liquor supermarket, with shopping carts, floor-standing pyramids of canned cocktail mixes and cases of beer, eight or ten checkout stations. Many of the customers are clearly on their way to the football stadium. I stare at their reflections in the tinted front windows, studying each person in one of the checkout lines until I realize that it's my line I'm looking at; I'm the suspicious man in the sunglasses with the two cases of beer balanced on the part of the shopping cart where the baby is supposed to be.

In the parking lot, Bill is reclining on the hood of the car, his back against the windshield, two white boxes of slides in his lap. I load the beer into the hatchback, turn the tape player on, hop up onto the hood with him.

He pretends to be a fraternity boy. "We got the car, we got the beer, we got the tunes," he says. "And we got the blimp. Look out, women."

We hold the slides to the sky. There it is, sailing through each frame like an apparition. Anything in the picture with the blimp seems comical, as if part of a montage. Bill himself is in some of them, a foreground face from a different realm. There are long shots, medium shots, close-ups of the silver ship.

"I want to see it again," I say. "In person, never mind on TV. Let's drive past the stadium and get a look at it."

Bill shakes his head and waves his hands. "We don't want to hassle with the stadium." He presses his wrist against my wrist as if to mingle blood. "Are we blimp brothers?" he says.

"Sure," I say. "Blimp brothers."

He winks. "I know where they keep it," he says. "At night."

When we get back, the cookout is already under way. Cars are parked all around the trailer, the stereo is playing, the barbecue pit is glowing on the lawn. People are dancing and playing volleyball. Rudy sees me and waves with a can of beer. He has his arm around Katy's shoulders; they're doing a kick dance to the music on the stereo. They dance over to where I'm loading the new beer into a garbage can full of ice.

"You got a real good woman here, son," Rudy says. "I might have to steal her away from you."

Katy laughs and bumps Rudy with her hip.

"Looks like she's already gone, Rudy," I say. I smile at Katy. She frowns.

"Hear that, honey?" Rudy says. "He's letting you go. He's turning you over to me."

"Hey, Rudy," I say. "I'm just curious. You ever heard of the Mayas?"

"The Mayas? Is that a rock group? Is that what's playing now? All this stuff sounds the same to me. I'd dance to anything with this little ballet star here." He gives Katy a hug.

"And you're looking real good on those dances, Rudy," I say.

"Son," Rudy says, "dance all you can now while you got the chance. I know you don't believe it, but someday your legs are gonna hurt when you get up in the morning. And keep drinking that stuff, so you can have one of these." He pats his belly.

I toss him a fresh can of beer. "Saint Francis of Assisi used to call his body Brother the Ass."

"He got that one right," Rudy says.

Katy points at me. "He's Saint Francis of Assisi," she says. "He said that."

Rudy grins and looks back and forth to see which one of us is putting him on.

"I'm not the real Saint Francis of Assisi," I say. "But the real Saint Francis has been an inspiration to me. People would ask him if he didn't get lonely wandering around all by himself, and he would say that he had a glorious and gracious lady by his side, and that her name was Poverty."

"I don't get it," Rudy says.

Katy runs her tongue over all her teeth; then she starts Rudy dancing again. "He's just being modest," she says. "He's the real Saint Francis of Assisi. He said those things."

"You can't fool her," Rudy says to me, dancing off.

I open a beer and dance into the trailer. People are lounging on Bill's Martian furniture, watching the game. On the television screen is a blimp shot from directly above the playing field. Seen from up there, football is almost comprehensible. During breaks in the action, there are shots of the blimp itself, poised over the stadium like a thought in a cartoon—as if all the people at the game are thinking the word "Goodyear," with a mythic winged foot separating the syllables.

In the kitchen, Wendy is standing at the counter slapping soyburger patties between her palms while Bill holds color slides in front of her face.

"Unreal," she says, bobbing her head to get the right light behind the slides. "Incredible. If you were a tribal people and this thing flew over, you'd worship it, right?"

"Definitely," Bill says.

Then Wendy notices me in the doorway.

"Saint Francis of Assisi," she says. "I hear you're a member of the blimp brigade."

"I'm one of the original blimp brothers," I say.

"I also hear you're one of the original nightmares to try to live with." She holds up a soyburger as if to throw it. "You and me are going to have a little talk, pal. About you in your big boots stomping around on the tender soul of my friend. You were supposed to think about somebody else for a change. You were supposed to make her life nicer, you weren't supposed to make it worse. I thought we discussed that. So how come she's a total wreck? What have you been doing in that apartment for the past year besides feeling sorry for yourself?"

I look at Bill. He's holding slides of the blimp in front of his eyes like dark glasses and pretending he's not here. Behind him I can see the birdbath through the bedroom window, the boy cherub peeing into the oyster shell, the beautiful birds frolicking about, the pasture, the sheep, the sky.

"That's not fair," I say. "Life isn't that simple. I've tried."

"Don't give me that," Wendy says.

"It takes two," I say.

The cookout still has plenty of party left in it when the sudden twilight is upon us. The days are much shorter than in the summertime—we'd all forgotten about that—and with the sun going down it's getting cold. Bill has the slide projector set up on the picnic table, a sheet draped over the clothesline for a screen.

I'm helping Katy put plastic forks and plates into a big green garbage bag. No mosquitoes are flying in our faces, no crickets are chirping. The birds have finished the hamburger rolls and flown away.

"These were good plastic forks, don't you think?" I say. "The heavy-gauge kind that don't break when you lay into the potato salad. Are they dishwasher safe? Maybe we should take some of these home and use them again."

"They're disposable," Katy says. "You're supposed to throw them away. Why do you want to take home the garbage?"

"You're right. Same goes for these nice plates, I guess."

"Same for the plates."

"And they would just be more possessions we'd have to divide up."

"I didn't hear that."

"I think you're making a big mistake choosing Fletcher over Rudy." I gesture to the pasture and then to the trailer park behind us. "This could all be yours someday."

Katy laughs. "I haven't been asked," she says.

Rudy is down at the base of the lawn by the birdbath, peeing into the pasture with some of the other guys. They're singing a drinking song.

"Rudy's really ripped," I say.

"Rudy's a wonderful, sweet man," Katy says.

"So what if I simply forbid you to go to Florence?" I say. "What if I chain you to the bed and refuse to let you out? Or how about if I stow away in your trunk and go along as your research slave? You could pass me a plate of gruel every day while I sat in the basement typing your index cards."

"Those don't sound like very attractive options," she says.

Then Bill flips on the slide projector. The Goodyear blimp appears on the screen, flying over the same backyard we're standing in. People cheer. Bill is wearing a white plastic spaceman helmet and shooting a ray gun that makes sparks and an otherworldly, oscillating sound. He pretends Rudy is an alien and chases him around the lawn. Then Bill aims the gun at the sky and fires a few bursts. "We are not alone on this planet!" he announces.

"He's been smoking that pot," Rudy says to us.

This is true, but when we look, the blimp itself is up there in the darkening sky like a big electric bug, its display lights traveling the length of its belly—spelling out the score of the football game and then a plug for all-weather radials. A giant likeness of a tire rolls in colors across the lights. Everybody cheers and applauds.

"Wendy's going to do paintings of it," Katy says to me. "She's putting me in one of them."

"I already have a deposit on that one," Rudy says. "That one's already spoken for."

Katy smiles and puts her head on Rudy's shoulder. "We know where they park the blimp," she says to me. "We're going to see it. Want to come along?"

"I don't much care for blimps," I say.

"Oh, come on," Rudy says. "Be a sport."

It's seven or eight miles to the blimp, back up in the hills where we were this afternoon. Bill is driving with his helmet on, shooting his ray gun out the window for the caravan of friends that's following us. Rudy's in the passenger seat with Katy on his lap. I'm in the back seat with Wendy.

"Going to see old Brother Blimp, eh, Saint Francis?" Bill says, passing me a bottle of whiskey.

"Old Brother Blimp," I say.

"Saint Francis of Assisi would have loved the Goodyear blimp," Wendy says, loading her camera. "He was kind of a tribal guy."

"He does love it," Katy says.

By the time we get to it, about a thousand people are already there. Cars are parked everywhere on either side of the road. I can't see anything until we get out and stand up.

Then I'm moved in a way I never was by any movie scene of the aliens landing their mother ship. The blimp is on top of a grassy hill in the meadow next to the road— stately, plump, big as the hill itself, floating with its nose attached to a mooring mast. It seems generous of the blimp to cooperate and be captured this way by the tiny people.

Its running lights are flashing across the landscape like lightning but in colors, bouncing the great silhouette in and out of focus against the dark horizon. Somehow, without being told, all the people approaching the blimp have formed two single-file lines to its nose and tail. Nobody climbs the hill except on one of those two streams of quiet pilgrims. We're on the line for the tail. It's really cold now, and in the colored light you can see everybody's breath escaping in little clouds.

Katy catches up to me and takes my arm. "Everything's gonna be all right," she says. "Things'll work out."

We look at each other for a minute, face to face.

"Wasn't a saint sent down to make sure the birds have a bath?" She gives me a kiss. "Wasn't a blimp sent down to reward him? Have a little faith, OK?"

"OK," I say. "Will do. Check. Roger."

She giggles and slaps me on the back. Then she slips and falls down on the dewy grass and gets up laughing. "I guess I've had some whiskey," she says.

When we get to the top, Rudy is there, getting the low-down from a Goodyear technician in blue coveralls. "This isn't the only one," Rudy says to us. "They have a whole fleet of these babies."

He's finding out how many cubic feet of helium go into a blimp like this, how many square yards of two-ply Dacron you need to make the skin. Rudy was in farm equipment before he retired; he likes the technical aspects of things.

"You guys could've kept her with me," he says. "I got a nice pasture closer to town."

"We don't like to be too close to town," the technician says.

A heavy rope is dangling from the tail, and Rudy goes right up and pulls on it. The whole blimp comes closer to the ground, which surprises even Rudy. We hunker down beneath the enormousness of it. When Rudy lets the rope go, all two hundred feet of blimp bounce back up into the air. It makes us gasp, and, as we're gasping, Bill nudges Katy and me out into the clearing below the cabin of the ship. He raises the visor on his spaceman helmet and fires a blast with his ray gun.

"I always knew your people would visit my people," he says to the Goodyear crew.

Laughter bubbles through the dark crowd all around us. Even the stern technicians chuckle and let us be.

"Hold hands now, lovebirds," Bill says to Katy and me.

We laugh in a groaning way and cover our eyes, and then uncover them and look at each other. We're embarrassed, but it would only make it worse not to play along. We hold hands and stand there shivering. Across the clearing beneath the blimp, Wendy is taking our photograph.

"Is this it?" Katy says. "Am I getting married now?" She laughs and staggers a bit. "Rudy, you're a witness to this. Bill, are you ordained?"

Bill fires another blast with the ray gun. "I have here two sample earthlings," he announces. "They have not been happy on this planet and have volunteered to leave. I offer them in exchange for information about your world. Take us to your leader."

MUSEUM OF LOVE

Love's museum is vain and foolish as the
Catacombs, where grinning apes and abject lizards
are embalmed, as, forsooth, significant of some
imagined charm.

—Melville, *Pierre*

" '*People grieve and bemoan* themselves,' "
said Mitchell, tossing off another shot of peppermint
schnapps, " '*but it is not half so bad with them as they
say.*' " He glanced around the room at the little group assembled there; then he drained his other glass of its chaser
of beer. His fellows followed suit. " '*The only thing grief
has taught me is to know how shallow it is.*' Ralph Waldo
Emerson."

"There you go, buddy," Ron put in. "Transcendence. A
new sense of the self." He extended his arms in a blessing
over Edgar's little house, formerly Edgar and Stephanie's
little house. Mitchell and Ron and Dave were there on a
mission of commiseration.

"She's gone," said Dave. "You gotta face it, boy. It's
over." He slashed a finger across his throat. "Over."

Slumped in his chair, schnapps and beer a fierce chemistry within him, Edgar gazed into the faces of his friends. He was asking himself a question. Are Mitchell, Ron, and Dave now my only companions, their wit, wisdom, and drunken camaraderie all the human succor available to me now? He swept his eyes across the living room full of memories. "I can't live here anymore!" was all he could exclaim.

They couldn't deny it. Edgar was a man of no small gifts, but the breadwinner he hadn't been. Stephanie, a daughter of old and new money, had walked out with the funds. Under no circumstances could Edgar afford to stay in the little house, or even to take a small studio in town. Times were hard. A discussion of real estate ensued amid the clink and slosh of another round.

Edgar covered his eyes with his fingers, put his thumbs in his ears. Still, the firelight and lamplight confirmed the persistence of a red-and-yellow world on the other side of his hands. He heard muddy murmurs of "seller's market," "money's tight," "location, location, location." It was his friends, Mitchell, Ron, and Dave. One third of a decent softball team for which he himself covered first; sensible, educated young men with their heads above water. And oafs. Wondrous oafs and boors.

I can't live here anymore! was the cry of property poisoning, not property lust—a warrior whoop against the house and its miasma of *things* advancing on Edgar's memory like the smoke from the cigarettes Stephanie had rolled out of black pipe tobacco in a little machine, inhaled with relish, and blown in people's faces, her most concise gesture of contempt for the parents (noted lung surgeon, wrinkled social creature) who paid for her pleasure. They paid for the little house, too. It took Stephanie two years of cohabitation therein to arrive at the idea that Edgar, her lover, was but another instrument of defiance, a powerful cigarette of sorts, and she got righteous one day the previous week and decided to quit. Cold turkey. To save both their lives, as she put it. A satchel over her shoulder and away in the car, without even taking her stuff.

Without even taking her stuff. When he blurted "I can't live here anymore!" Edgar had meant that he couldn't continue to live in the very rooms where he'd loved as no man had loved before, besieged at every step by the personal effects of a woman who would float like a ghost through all his days until death. The other issue, that of not being permitted to remain in the little house and having nowhere else to go, had not, in the heat of heartbreak, occurred to him. He removed his hands from around his head. Someone was calling his name.

"Edgar," said Ron, "are you listening to me? What was said about the disposition of the house, the selling of it or the assumption of the mortgage?"

Edgar looked at them blankly. The events of that day were a muddle of evil.

"Try to remember, Edgar."

He remembered. "She said I would hear from her father."

His friends made low whistles of awe. "Edgar, you had a hot one," Mitchell said.

These words put Edgar freshly in mind of his loss. He rose from his chair and clutched the mantel of the fireplace, where lay a collection of colorful stones and shells. "We found these on the beach at Key West!" He swept them to the floor, staggered to the window, wrapped the blue batik drapery around his head. "She made these curtains by hand. I remember the day! Stephie! *Stephanie!*"

His friends whispered among themselves. Edgar, poor Edgar. On the diamond in their minds they saw trouble at first base—weakness, preoccupation, a foot not on the bag. Dave gave Edgar a brotherly hug, took away the satin ballet slipper he was pressing to his lips. "Grip on yourself, boy."

"Everywhere I look! Everything I see!"

They installed him on the sofa, held a schnapps beneath his nose. Mitchell patted Edgar's head. "Your own house feels like a mummy's tomb, doesn't it, pal? Every object a token of the life that's gone."

Edgar took a sip of the schnapps and nodded his dismal agreement. Mitchell's mind was a piercing thing. In silence they pondered the dark ramifications. Ron tried to lighten things up.

"Hey, man," he said, jostling one of Edgar's knees. "Maybe that's the answer! You could charge admission to the place, solve all your money problems!" Nearly everyone laughed. Edgar seemed actually to consider the idea, or else he was drifting away again. Ron kept shaking his knee.

"Edgar," Dave said. "What *did* Stephanie say about all her things? She must have said something."

Edgar raised himself up and struggled to recall. His face went rubbery as it broke in upon him. "She said I could have a yard sale!" he cried, and crumpled onto the coffee table.

They put him to bed. Dave said, "Edgar, are you listening to me? Whatever you decide to do, you should make the first move. Don't sit here like a chump waiting for the old man's emissaries to show up. He'll probably have the constable serve notice on you, the bastard, ordering you to quit the premises. Beat 'em to the punch. Clear out now, force them to deal with all her stuff. Got me?"

Edgar threw up into a wastepaper basket.

" 'Better to have loved and lost—' " burbled Mitchell, but the others clapped hands upon his mouth and dragged him to the door, Dave giving a final thumbs-up sign to the rumpled form of Edgar, lying there.

The telephone was ringing. Edgar unslumbered himself to answer it. He had been in the jungle, in a dream, on safari with Stephanie. Tribesmen had captured them and made her a goddess. Edgar, tied up, was being carried to a kettle steaming on a fire. Stephanie was waving goodbye. A chieftain was jangling a bell to summon his distant kin to a feast. A woman from the State Historical Society was on the phone.

"Someone on our staff is quite interested in your proposal," she was saying, "and would like to visit you, today if possible, to discuss it."

"Today," Edgar said. He tried to disentangle his body from humid ropes of bedclothes and lingerie. Something else was wound around his mind. His proposal.

There was a pause. "Miss Price would like an appointment for two this afternoon."

Edgar glanced at his watch. It was eleven o'clock. The house looked like a metaphor for psychosis. "OK," he said.

"Very good. One other thing. She asks that you not do

any rearranging on her account, or remove any objects, or in any way alter the appearance of the dwelling."

The disinfection of his person occupied the remainder of the morning. Then he was ravenous and had to eat, and then he rushed around the rooms trying to flatten the highest peaks of the house's departure from tidiness. He didn't get far. The crushed gravel of the horseshoe drive popped and crackled beneath the tires of an auto. Edgar peeped out. It was a low-slung red sports car—Italian, he thought—from which a tall, dark woman was emerging chickwise, as from an egg. Miss Price's great beauty was plainly discernible. He opened the door and waved hello. She came beaming up the walk with a briefcase and a Polaroid.

"I love it already!" she exclaimed, extending her hand. "Katherine Price, from the Historical Society, new curatorial projects department. Friends call me Kitty."

Edgar shook hands and introduced himself.

Kitty said, "I've been looking through our books. Did you know your house was the servants' quarters? The mansion was over there. It burned down about forty years ago. Your garage was the carriage house."

The realtor had told Edgar and Stephanie these things. "I think this place is about a hundred and fifty years old," he said.

"A hundred and sixty-seven," Kitty said. She followed him inside. The disarray was quite unlike simple slovenliness. "Now, don't say a word. Don't tell me a thing about her. I want to feel the life in the artifacts."

Kitty wandered around, humming to herself, snapping things with the Polaroid. Edgar tagged along, sheepish, at a distance, vague shame inflating like a surgical balloon in his heart. To judge by where she lingered and snapped, Kitty had an uncanny sense for the emotional charge on physical things. She sniffed out the mementos that laid Edgar open like knives.

"You two collected these together, didn't you?" she asked, snapping a picture of the stones and shells from the beach at Key West. Edgar had restored them to the mantelpiece before she arrived. "On a romantic journey to the sea?" Sadly, he nodded his head. "When love was young?" He nodded more emphatically. A long, trembly sigh from deep down escaped him.

Kitty shot the blue batik curtains, then held one of them up by its jagged, amateurish hem. "Touching." Stepping away for a better angle, she noticed the pink toe of a ballet slipper poking out from beneath the sofa. She looked at Edgar; her eyes contained galaxies of knowledge and pity. "A thousand words," she said, taking the slipper's picture. "No, a million." Making her circuit of the study, she came upon Stephanie's pipe tobacco and papers and rolling machine. "What have we here, a little contraband?"

Edgar explained.

"She rolled her own cigarettes out of black pipe tobacco? To spite her mom and dad? What a woman this was!" She snapped them.

Edgar lowered himself softly onto a chair, needing to close his eyes for a spell. He was having sensations from his boyhood—of being caught in some monstrous apparatus, of having failed to look very deeply into things. He conceived the scheme of quieting himself and then throwing open his eyes onto Kitty and the house and the absence of Stephanie, thus literally to look deeply and perceive in a flash the true nature of his circumstances. He threw open his eyes. Kitty was gone. He bustled upstairs. She was in the bedroom, photographing the interior of Stephanie's walk-in closet.

Edgar wandered over to the window and stared down at the garden he and Stephanie had sown. A plunge from that modest height into the furrowed loam would not ensure the end of his affairs, unless by chance a tomato stake were driven through his bosom. He sat down on the bed. Kitty had lapsed into the rapture of the boutique, feeling her way through the bureau and closet and redwood chest full of Stephanie's clothes, holding certain items up against herself, most of which were a little too small. At length she turned to Edgar, hands on her hips, Polaroid dangling by its strap from her wrist. "I know this woman!" she announced.

"You do?" Edgar's blood bubbled around his bones. "You know Stephanie?"

"Oh, I don't mean I actually know her. I mean I know who she is when I see her things, and what she must have meant to you. Who you were together!" She sat next to Edgar on the bed. "Poor, poor fellow. Going through such agony here in the house you shared with her." She combed his hair with her fingers, gestured to the space around them. "The play of these images like a planetarium of pain." Edgar ventured to rest his head on Kitty's shoulder. Abruptly she stood up, reanimated, and traipsed back down the stairs.

Edgar found her photographing the dining appointments and Stephanie's high-tech kitchen gadgetry. He expressed his regrettable ignorance of curatorial studies.

"No false modesty!" she remonstrated, tweaking his cheek. "Credit where credit's due. You may not know the literature, but your instincts are astonishing. And in the middle of a nasty ordeal! When they told me what you'd proposed on the phone, the genius of it gripped me at once. The museum of a love affair, indeed. It's inspired!"

Edgar shuffled his feet and tried to appear humble. It was strangely easy. "It really has potential, then? It's a good idea?"

"It's a great idea, Edgar. A curatorial dream. What we're always looking for, those of us in the profession who are thinking progressively: a new approach, a fresh way to depict perennial human experience with a display of objects, while capturing the spirit of a particular age. The zeitgeist."

She pulled the cord on Stephanie's centrifugal washer-dryer for salad greens. It spun for a minute and stopped.

"We work with collections of things that evoke a legendary past, however recent or remote. But museums as most people think of them, big buildings full of objets d'art and open to the public, are a relatively recent phenomenon, maybe two hundred years old. Before that, collections of valuable things were assembled by private individuals—the result, usually, of the hoarding instinct. War is always good for that, or any time of economic uncertainty."

Some great calamity, thought Edgar. Turmoil. Distortion of value.

"The very earliest collections of objects, though, were associated with places of worship. Magic collections, we call them. On display for the faithful. The light of reason, intellectual curiosity, even esthetics and understanding of the past—none of that had anything to do with it. These were power objects, Edgar. Medievalism was the fullest expression of it. The medieval response to antiquity was fear. When some peasant was plowing his field and turned up a pagan artifact, his first step was to call a priest, who bricked the thing up into a wall of the church so it couldn't give anybody the evil eye. And they loved the relics of martyrs and saints, of course. They staged massive expeditions for holy stuff that could heal wounds and cure diseases. The Benedictine monastery at Vendôme in France owned a vial containing a tear wept by Jesus at the death of Lazarus. Skeletons were the hottest items. At one point, nineteen churches claimed to have the jawbone of John the Baptist."

The wild things people used to believe in, Edgar thought. Well, it's behind us now. On with the enlightenment.

Kitty smiled and tapped the windowsill above the kitchen sink. A tiny bird's nest was resting there, with a broken blue egg inside it. "What's this?" she asked.

"Bird's nest. Stephanie found it in the woods one day."

"But now it's on your windowsill. Why did she feel compelled to bring it into the house? Think about it."

"Because it looks nice?"

"Because it's a power object, Edgar—architecture that would be here if people never were. A vessel, a home, a place to feed babies and watch them fly away. It meant one thing for Stephanie when she found it in the woods. It means something else now, here on display. You look at that and tell me it's just nice to look at."

Edgar looked at it. There was the rustle of leaves beneath his feet, Stephanie's hand holding his hand. A sweatered shoulder against his cheek, nip of teeth on his ear. Her little cry when she saw the nest lying on the ground. . . . Edgar grabbed it from the windowsill and pressed it to his breast. *"Stephanie!"*

"Careful, careful." Kitty took the nest away and gave Edgar a sisterly hug. "And these pebbles on the mantelpiece over here?"

Edgar followed her to the living room. "Power objects?"

"Magic stones. They were the rage in the Middle Ages. People who couldn't afford expensive relics could always find a few magic stones lying around. A man would wait until his wife was asleep and then put a magic stone on her head to elicit confessions of infidelity. A little late for that, in your case. Also, warriors carried them in their mouths when they went into battle." She placed a stone on Edgar's tongue. "Feel anything?"

"I do feel a little something," he mumbled.

"Of course you do. Now, the Renaissance and Reformation turned all this around. Spirit of rational inquiry, beauty and proportion, Calvin against the veneration of relics. A great leap, certainly, but there was something of the-baby-out-with-the-bathwater about it. These things persist as human needs, Edgar. In Boston, the Christian Science plaza dwarfs Symphony Hall across the street where the mind music of Bach is played. You go tell them there's no such thing as faith healing. Anyway, that was my dissertation topic: 'Excluded Middle: The Place of Vestigial Medievalism in Contemporary Collections.' "

Edgar always felt humbled in the presence of sweeping erudition. He sucked his stone reflectively, musing over the proposal he'd summoned up out of schnapps and self-pity and the instinct to survive. Somehow he wasn't following through. He spit his stone into his hand. "How does this all relate to my museum?" he asked.

"It relates completely!" Kitty said. "What you have here would fall into the newest category of all, the Historical House Museum. It's becoming more popular all the time and seems to be exempt from the problems that plague other sorts of museums. An eco-museum, the French would call it—whatever's there when you find it. People just love to visit them. And what could capture that magical sense of objects—the impulse behind the earliest collections—better than the power of a loved one's possessions for the lover she spurned? The living record of a doomed affair! It's romance and history and beauty and fate. What everyone wants and no one understands. The oldest kind of museum wedded to the newest kind. A truly American contribution . . . and my first work on my own in the field! Edgar, I'm incredibly excited about this project!"

Two days later Kitty called.

"Edgar! We pushed it through! It's approved!"

Kitty, Edgar thought, has some considerable clout. "It only took two days to get it approved?"

"They loved it. Her wealth and hauteur, your bohemian radicalism. Historic house concept, changing social patterns, new significance of individual lives, emotional resonance of our era. Plus, Grandpa founded the Historical Society."

"Ah."

"A work crew is coming tomorrow first thing."

"Um, Kitty?"

"Yes?"

"Will I be able to, you know, stay here, like I always did?"

"Stay there? Like you always did? That's the whole point! You living in the house, just like it was. With one conspicuous absence, of course, which provides the creative tension for the viewers. The source of their dialogue with the place. They have to feel Stephanie's presence in her artifacts."

"Right, right. But I mean, will I have to pay rent?"

"Rent? No, silly! The state has acquired the house. It's a museum now. It was your idea, after all. You're a big part of it!"

Edgar thought he felt much relieved.

In the morning, the work crew arrived, Kitty's red car not far behind. She emerged in blue jeans, sneakers, scarf on her head, man's shirt tied in a knot at her waist. She was personally supervising the labors of the crew. Edgar was wearing his blue jeans too. Kitty put him on the payroll as a consultant. "It's our baby!" she said.

Under Kitty's direction, the workers toiled like happy demons. To Edgar they seemed a blur of ponytails and beards, cut-offs and T-shirts, a collective pulse of jocular energy in the service of Kitty's ideas. Edgar wished he were just a member of the happy crew and not the petrified focus of its efforts. But I've been given the nod by history, he thought. Called to a higher destiny.

The garage was cleaned out, its interior painted white, track lighting and display cases installed. It was being turned into the Before Each Other Room, one of Kitty's innovations. She and Edgar scoured the house for all the old stuff from before he and Stephanie met: their baby pictures, crayon drawings, high school rings and sweaters; yearbooks, scrapbooks, a corsage from one of Stephanie's proms. Edgar wondered who had been her date; he hadn't seen the corsage before, nor most of the things in all those boxes in the basement. There were packets of letters, tied with ribbon and colorful yarn, to and from young fellows she'd never mentioned.

When the Before Each Other Room was finished, Kitty walked Edgar through on a practice tour. They stood before the display case—one out of ten—devoted to him. In the light of the new lamps he looked at his old things under glass. The identification labels, so professional-looking, startled him. He saw EDGAR'S LITTLE-LEAGUE BASEBALL MITT and broke down badly.

"Edgar, Edgar," Kitty said, patting him on the back, trying to buck him up. "You have to be stronger than that. Anyway, there's only this room and one other formal display. The house proper stays just the way it was, except cleaned up and arranged a little bit."

Edgar made a gruesome face: eyes squeezed shut, lips curled over his teeth. Kitty reminded him that the power of objects was a neutral force, either for good or ill, harm or healing. It was right to be moved, but it was wrong to be a weakling. There was enormous strength and comfort to be had, she said, in giving oneself over to the continuity of things. Maybe the most wonderful windfall of all, she reasoned, was the therapeutic potential of the museum for Edgar himself, the rare chance to evoke his past systematically and know it as of a piece—to really inhabit the dark interstices of time. Did he know that "curatorial" shared its etymology with "curative"?

"Think of it, Edgar. How many people get an opportunity like this?" Edgar nodded vaguely. "And you won't be alone! Every day you'll see lots of people who want to re-construct it right along with you. People from all walks of life who want to stroll through your little house and feel the collision of desire and destiny. And I'll be there, of course."

"You will?"

"When I conduct the tours, certainly. Three times a day, Tuesday through Saturday, an hour-and-a-half per tour of the house and grounds, with an hour off between tours. Other than that you won't be disturbed."

"Oh."

"The rest of the time all your own, to do all the things you want to do, and no worries about a job. Edgar, you're a very lucky guy."

OPENING DAY said the cloth banner draped across the front of the house, hand-sewn by Kitty, shades of Betsy Ross. A permanent sign was mounted on the lawn, lettered in a clean, conservative typeface. MUSEUM OF LOVE, it said. Where the old mansion had been was a parking lot. Many cars were parked there.

Edgar could hear commotion, the sound of excited voices and feet. Kitty's first tour had tramped through the garden and grounds, lingered in the Before Each Other Room. Now they were coming into the house. Kids were running around. *"Mothers! Control your children!"* he heard the muffled voice of Kitty say. Then, in the relative calm, she began her prepared remarks. The shuffling and murmuring of the tourists obscured some of what she said; the house itself absorbed much of the rest. Still, Edgar could infer enough: it was the part about Stephanie's wealth and hauteur, his bohemian radicalism. *"Storybook romance,"* filtered through to him, *"star-crossed lovers," "his dilettantism, the fruits of which the world will never see," "black pipe tobacco," "satin ballet slippers."*

The visitors moved across the house in a mass, looking at the things, cooing in wonder. *"Left one day without a word of warning, leaving everything she had, making this museum possible."* He heard gasps of disbelief. *"They were to be married in the fall."* It was a lie, but a powerful one. The crowd groaned in a body.

The deep vibrations of the house changed in pitch and timbre; Kitty was taking the tour upstairs. Edgar heard humming that must have been excited voices—the reaction, he supposed, to Stephanie's wardrobe. Some of the nicer items had been laid out across the bed. It seemed a great while before the tour clumped back down to ground level, and then Edgar heard the increasing volume of their enthusiasm; the museum was a big success. The group assembled at length before the basement door, where Kitty stood waiting to speak. Edgar pictured her there—glowing, patrician, her posture perfect. In the anticipatory hush, he heard her announce the final display, "One man's response to deep mystery and loss." He'd asked her to leave that part out. The key she wore on a chain around her wrist unlocked the basement door. She threw it open.

Light from upstairs ran down the steps. In it, Kitty appeared, leading the way, enjoining the viewers to hold the banister. She wore stockings, heels, a navy cotton suit over lacy white blouse. Her dark hair swept across her shoulders. Kitty is certainly a lovely woman, Edgar thought. The crowd collected at the bottom of the stairs. Kitty guided the tour along the damp stone walls of the cellar, past the old coal bin and the ancient furnace that all the kids said looked like a big, spooky monster, with its many arms reaching up into the house.

Edgar couldn't make out faces in the dimness, but he heard the singular catching of breath when they saw a man in a pin-striped suit—white shirt, dark tie, carnation in his lapel—sitting in the corner in a bentwood rocker. In his lap was a negligee that he wrung between his hands. "It's the suit he would have worn to the altar," Kitty declared. It was too much; he'd told her so. The crowd made a low and awful moan. "The rocking chair belonged to Stephanie's grandmother." That much was true. Kitty drew the visitors closer.

Above his head and to either side, spotlights played on plaster niches built against the basement wall. In the central niche was a photograph of Stephanie and Edgar, taken on their trip to Greece; in the left, Stephanie's favorite African violet. The third niche contained a tiny bird's nest in which was a broken blue egg and a lock of Stephanie's hair. Polaroid snapshots were fastened around the perimeter of each niche. Kitty made authoritative remarks on the history of museums, various curatorial approaches to the past, the uses of power objects through the ages. At his cue, the part about magic stones, Edgar thrust out his tongue to show the pebbles resting there. "Our two lovers found those on the beach at Key West," Kitty told the tourists.

Elderly heads of coiffed blue hair bobbed in front of Edgar's face. Pop-eyed kids stared, transfixed, at the stones; it was the best thing they'd ever seen, Edgar could tell. He felt a certain pride. Some of the ladies began to cry, and Edgar did battle with the power of suggestion. He reinstalled his tongue, bit down hard on the stones to fortify himself. It seemed only to encourage the burning water that sprang from his head. He reached up to wipe his face with the negligee, but Kitty rushed over and stayed his hand. Through the blur, Edgar noticed her rummaging in her bag. For a handkerchief, he thought, God bless her. In her smile he saw appreciation beyond words. Her hand touched his cheek; she whispered "You're beautiful" in his ear. She was holding a little glass vial beneath his eye.

PURIFICATION

T*he natives have many legends* about this long, finger-shaped lake I'm floating on with Leo, my father-in-law, the two of us fishing from a borrowed power-boat on the sparkling silver-green water. The most famous lake legend says that a gigantic monster lives at the bottom. When I came here five years ago to teach painting at the college, the local Loch Ness creature was the first thing I heard about this place, though it hasn't been sighted for a century now. But another old piece of lore claims that the lake has no bottom at all, and this one is more than a folk tale. It's a fact that nobody has ever found the bottom of it. The lake was gouged into the earth by glaciers, like its sisters fanned across this region. On a map, they do resemble the fingers of a hand, but this is the cold and deep one. Our lake is so deep that the Navy secretly tested submarines here during World War Two, and *they* never found the bottom.

Leo's not the type for legends and myths, but he's joined me in letting them explain the rotten luck we've had this weekend. The monster has awoken and eaten all the fish, we've been saying to each other. Or: The fish must have swum down to the other side of the world, all the way through to China.

"Don't tell me my magic blue spoon's not working," he says to me now, looking over his shoulder at my lure coming up out of the water. He's casting south of our boat and I'm casting north, which means I face the distant head of the lake where the town has its municipal park and beach. The plan is to fish our way up there through the day, and then meet our wives in the park for a Memorial Day picnic.

"The milfoil likes your magic blue spoon," I tell Leo, reeling the lure all the way up. Nothing's on it but clumps of the bristly underwater plant that grows like crazy from the shallows out to the drop-off a hundred yards from shore.

Leo shakes his head. "A spoon like that usually drives lake trout wild," he says.

The blue spoon is the third or fourth lure I've used so far today. It looks enticing enough to me. I can't imagine being a fish and not chasing this sparkly thing. I clean it off and zing it out to a peaceful-looking patch of water. It wobbles wonderfully as I reel it back, calling out to fish everywhere. But after another four or five casts, I've only hooked more gobs of the underwater plant.

"If they were having a water-milfoil contest, we'd be the winners, Pop."

"We are the winners," he says.

This is the third day in a row we've been out here, and our last, and we haven't caught one decent fish. I thought I had a good strike our first morning, but it got away, and then Leo landed a rock bass so tiny it made us feel sad. And that's been it. Even I—not much of a fisherman—have caught a few good ones on outings over the years. But this weekend, for some reason, they're not biting. We've tried live bait, and they don't even steal it. Every summer since Beth and I settled here, Leo has wanted to come up and fish this lake, and every year he's been so tied up with business or courts and lawyers that he couldn't take the time. Now he's finally here, and we're disgracing ourselves. And this was his last chance.

"Let's scoot out more toward the middle, Leo," I say, laying down my pole. We've been fishing the edge of the lake and tolerating the weeds because the trout are supposed to be in shallow water this time of year, staying warm. Clearly they're not, or maybe they think our colorful lures are a puppet show we're putting on for them.

"Get a more direct line to China," Leo replies, smiling around the unlit cigar he starts chomping on as soon as his wife and daughter are out of sight.

The lake is only about a mile wide at this point, but it's a good forty-five miles long, and as we dislodge ourselves from the shoreline, the sheer extent of the water reveals itself—a vast blue cut in the land, running south all the way to the horizon. Of all the things people say about this lake, this is the most true: how tremendously beautiful it really is. Near the middle I throttle down and shut off the motor, and we drift in the sudden quiet.

Many other boats are strewn about today, most of them bearing fisherfolk out trying their luck. A few miles north I see our town and its waterworks, a brick building on the shore where they lace lake water with chlorine and then pump the bad-tasting result to every citizen. In the other direction I see the stunning vineyards where our famous wine grapes are grown. Starting about ten miles south of town, the banks of the lake are lined with these regimented parcels of land. In the winter they look almost like cemeteries for soldiers—the vacant trellises suggesting rows of burial plots, the bare woody grapevines like simple crosses. Just now the pale spring leaves are changing to a dark, shiny green. In any season the vineyards and water make this lake country as fine, I think, as Tuscany or the south of France. I've painted them many times, and I hadn't done a landscape for years before moving here.

But there's a catch to the pretty vineyards. Every year their runoff sends great quantities of pesticides and fertilizer into all these glacial lakes. That's one of the reasons for our notorious chlorination. The fertilizer force-feeds the water milfoil, producing the massive fronds that scrub your boat like a car wash as you cast off from shore. Old-timers remember milfoil as a sparse, tiny plant in the days before agribusiness. As to the pesticides, Leo says they're bad but they don't explain the dioxin and PCBs in the internal organs of our fish. Industrial pollution is the culprit there, he says; it could be coming from anywhere, but coming it is. In my five years here, the state has issued increasingly stern warnings about consuming creatures from the waters of this region. From our particular lake—not yet as bad as some others—it's supposed to be safe to eat one fish per month. Beth, nearly seven months pregnant, won't even let us bring one in the house. Not that it seems likely we will.

"This is a sad state of affairs for the Lake Trout Capital of the World," Leo laughs now, reeling back his empty lure from the deeper water.

He's referring to our most recent local legend—an invention of the Chamber of Commerce, I suspect, since few fishermen seem to think we really are the Lake Trout Capital of the World. But as you drive into town on the lake road, you see a billboard welcoming you to just that: a large green fish breaking the painted water beneath the proclamation, the line in its mouth running back to a tiny sportsman in a distant boat. Every Memorial Day weekend, the town holds its Lake Trout Tournament, a three-day competition with a handsome prize. The tournament ends today, and we're in it.

A decade ago, when Leo and Betty were in their mid-fifties, he gave up a nice, secure life and tried to save the world. That's what I call it when I tease him about what he did. He would never put it that way. Leo is an engineer. He says he was pursuing engineering solutions to engineering problems. He would never admit to anything as glorious as trying to save the world. Purifying the world was what Leo tried to do, but at that late hour of our dirty history, purifying and saving amounted to the same thing.

He went to school on the GI Bill, then had a long career as a project manager for a firm that made high-tech medical equipment. In the med-tech business, Leo supervised the invention of machines that could show your insides on color TV, look at unborn babies, even remove a person's kidney stones—all without lifting a knife. I think of his achievements as heroic stuff, but the success is probably why he got bored doing it. Leo is the kind of person who needs to be irritated by something, and success isn't irritating. Eventually, something else was going to get his goat, and what finally got it was our environment. Pollution didn't just ruin Leo's cherished fishing and camping places, make animals extinct, cause the cancers that his own equipment revealed. Pollution offended his sense of order. The earth was a machine, in Leo's mind, and if you turned the rain into acid or punched holes in the ozone, you were grossly misusing a machine. And it looked to Leo like nobody was doing anything about it. His colleagues seemed to be sitting on their hands.

The day his irritation got the better of him, Leo quit his job and started a company of his own. I met him when his venture was a few years old, my new girlfriend's intense technologist father. By the time Beth and I got married, two years later, Leo's engineers had filed for important patents in pollution control, and his business was starting to fly. And then his bad luck arrived, masquerading as good. His small purification company caught the eye of a gigantic chemical conglomerate. They wanted to make Leo one of their subsidiaries. They promised him control of product development, and they promised a fortune for R & D. Leo saw their money as the way to do what he'd set out to do, and he accepted their offer. It took the giant corporation less than a year to force him out.

He's spent the three years since then in courts and lawyers' offices suing for breach of contract, trying to regain rights to patents the conglomerate seems to have bought only to make sure they'll never be used. Leo would like to use them; the amazing man is ready to start all over again, but so far he's gotten nowhere.

Now, out on the lake, he reels his lure in again and examines his chewed-over cigar. "So how are we doing?" he asks me. "Are the Plaintiffs catching any fish out here?"

"Not that I know of, Pop," I say. Calling us the Plaintiffs has been one of Leo's little jokes this weekend. I give my line a little tug to see if maybe a fish latched on and then fell asleep. It's been a couple of minutes since I took my last cast and forgot to reel it back. No, nothing's on.

I look back toward shore to see how I became the other half of Leo's joke. There they are—the towers of the college crowning the hill. This was the year I came up for tenure there. I had the blessings of my department, not to mention solid votes on the faculty's tenure committee. I was entitled to hopefulness. I'd taught and painted well, got myself taken on by a good gallery in New York. I'd kept my side of the bargain. But that wasn't the point. In four years I'd seen the best young professors get their walking papers, one right after another. Office hallways were beginning to feel like corridors of ghosts, every third doorway the marker of a good colleague who'd disappeared. And it was for this reason, after two miscarriages in as many years, that Beth and I decided to stop trying to have a kid until we saw how things went with my job.

By the time I was denied tenure this spring, her pregnant belly was blossoming nicely beneath her blouse. On campus I've become a cause célèbre. The tenure committee voted me in, and I had a week of congratulations—until the Board of Trustees overruled their recommendation, citing my incompatibility with the ideals of the college. My outraged colleagues wrote letters to the Board, stood up to protest at faculty meetings, got me a lawyer who says it's the tightest case he's ever seen. Students signed petitions and hung a banner for me across the front of the administration building. The people inside that building aren't talking, but I know what they think. They expect summer to dry the whole thing up. They figure my support will erode and I'll lose the heart to fight. They've done this before and I haven't, and they're not stupid people.

"Hey, Leo, I just had an idea," I say.

He has a cast in process, spinning rod cocked back behind his shoulder. He lets it whip with that eerie ratcheting sound. The lure arcs up and out about fifty feet and plops where he thinks a big old trout may be lurking. "Yeah? What's that?"

"I'll jump in the lake and bite your line, and then you can enter me in the competition."

He laughs so hard it blows the cigar right out of his mouth. It floats a few feet away, brown plug in blue-green, its shredded end inking the water like a squid. "Now look what you made me do," he says.

It's six o'clock when we glide into the park at the head of the lake and tie up at one of the municipal docks. We feel like Lake Trout Tournament victims—neither of us even had a nibble. But on the way up here we pulled alongside a few friendly looking vessels and saw the keepers other folks had caught. The town paper will have a winner on its front page tomorrow. Many anchored boats are bobbing about the marina now, and the park is full of people. Children are fishing from the piers or throwing Frisbees across the grass. We're hungry and water-weary, two men badly in need of a picnic. And we've come to the right place: I see Beth and Betty up among the trees, holding down a table and grill. They see us and wave, and when we climb out of the boat they're clopping down the tongue of wooden slats to meet us—Beth in her blue maternity sundress, Betty in a sunny yellow top and jeans.

We kiss our wives, and then I bend down to greet Beth's belly. "Hello there, Chardonnay," I say. It's our working title for the girl we're having in a couple of months. We can't seem to come up with anything else, and now it's begun to stick. We might go with it. She was conceived in wine country, after all. Betty thinks it's a scandal, our referring to our kid like she was hootch. "This is your father speaking," I say. "Paging Miss Chardonnay." We know she's a girl from the tests Beth had, just as we know she's another normal, undefective inheritor of the earth. And we're grateful. Sometimes Chardonnay kicks when I talk to her, but she's not coming in right now.

"So where are the fish?" Betty wants to know.

Leo and I glance down the fronts of ourselves, as though we might find fish clinging to our shirts.

"You didn't catch anything?" Betty says. "Either of you? Again?"

"The fish all have amnesia out there, Betty," I say. "They've forgotten they're fish. They see a tantalizing lure and they don't know what it is."

"Maybe it's a communication problem," Beth says.

"Maybe you should have attached a sign to your line. 'Fish, bite here,' it could have said."

Leo backhands my shoulder. "Why didn't you think of that? You're the professor."

We stroll together up the grassy slope to our picnic table.

"Has he been chewing on cigars all day?" Betty asks me.

"Not that I know of," I say.

Leo gives me a secret pinch. "Light that charcoal before I eat it, son," he says, installing himself on the chaise with a beer.

I pour the briquettes into the grill and give them a good dousing with the starter fluid. My mother-in-law is regarding me curiously. "Did I put too much rocket fuel on them, Betty?"

"No," she says. "I was just thinking how lucky you are."

"Only in love," I say, smiling at Beth. "I've only had this one great catch."

"Now what does that mean?" Betty says, suddenly upset. "I don't want to hear you talking like that. You'll find a new job and new ideas for paintings. Your daughter will have a wonderful life. You're the luckiest man in the world."

I look at Beth, and she looks away. They've covered all the major topics, it seems. "I meant the fishing, Betty. We didn't catch any fish. It was a joke." I drop a match into the charcoal, and up it goes.

"Oh, sorry. I thought you were being negative again."

"Again?"

She steps around the conflagration to give me a kiss. "I just meant we'd love you even if you became a bum."

"You're a bum right now," Leo says through the flames.

"Oh!" Betty says all at once. "We saw Dr. Spock on TV today. He tried to climb over the fence at that place down there, and they arrested him. Dr. Spock, on TV in handcuffs! I couldn't believe it. We raised Beth by that book, honey," she tells Leo.

"The demonstration at the depot," Beth says to me, a warning in her eye.

"Oh, that," I say. "That happens every Memorial Day. Did Dr. Spock get arrested this time? Good for him."

The fence Dr. Spock tried to climb surrounds the vast army depot ten miles south of here, the one thing our Chamber of Commerce doesn't advertise about this beautiful land of the lakes. The army will neither confirm nor deny what we all know about the place—that it contains the single largest cache of nuclear weapons in the world. There's a state park across the highway from the depot where big antinuclear demonstrations are held several times each year. Beth and I always attend at least one, us and ten or twenty thousand other people wearing buttons and carrying signs. We've never joined the small group of civil disobeyers who march across the highway, climb the fence, and get arrested. But even so, the depot protests became one of my troubles at the college. I was in the habit of telling my students about these events, giving a little pep talk about global destruction and encouraging them to turn out. Word of that got around, and I ended up in the Provost's office for a reading from the faculty handbook. I've done other bad things at the college too, though we haven't made a point of telling Leo and Betty about them.

"What's so good about Dr. Spock getting arrested?" Leo

wants to know, sipping his beer beside the smoking barbecue.

"He got arrested trying to save the world, Pop," I say.
"That's good in my book."

Beth fires me a wicked look, and I decide to let it drop. I
decide to be good, though it's difficult.

"You think we should just throw away our guns, right,
Barry?" Leo says. "And then sit back and see what the
other side decides to do?"

He knows perfectly well what I think. We've had this
discussion many times. "I think everybody should throw
their guns away," I say.

"But that's not gonna happen, Barry."

"We're never gonna find out, Leo."

"Barry," Beth says. "Please."

"I just don't want to see little Chardonnay grow up in a
dictatorship," Leo says.

"Me neither," I say.

"There," Betty says. "See? You agree on that."

"Maybe I'm touchy because it's Memorial Day," Leo
says. "I saw guys get killed, Barry."

"I know you did, Leo. And I didn't. I've never seen
anybody get killed, and I'm glad."

"There's a reason you didn't have to," he says. "And if
you did, you'd have a different idea of justice."

"I have a fine idea of justice," I say. "There isn't any."

"Oh, for God's sake," Beth says.

"I think there's justice," Leo says.

"After what's happened to you?"

"Sure. What there isn't is any guarantees. Life doesn't

come with guarantees. You've got the two things confused."

"What's that supposed to mean?" Beth says.

But I know what it means. I know what's coming.

"Well, take tenure for college professors," Leo says. "That's a guarantee, right? Somebody guaranteeing that you'll always have a job. That you'll never get kicked out of their club. That you'll never have to pick up the pieces and start over again. Who besides professors expects a guarantee like that?"

"Lawyers," I say.

"Right," Leo says, and nobody has to tell us what Leo thinks of lawyers.

"Leo," I say, "I completely agree with you on this one. I think tenure is bizarre. It's medieval and weird, and they use it to hurt people. I'm against the whole idea."

"But that was the deal," Beth says. "That was the game they said they'd play. And now they want to change the rules. You earned it, and you have to fight."

"Because they changed their own rules? It was corrupt from the beginning. Life doesn't come with guarantees, just like Leo said. They should do away with the whole thing."

"For the people in line after you," Betty says. "You can be the cut-off person."

"Are you telling me you're not going to fight this college about your job?" Beth says.

"I'm not telling you anything, babe."

Leo slaps his thighs and clambers up out of the chaise. "OK, the Plaintiffs are gonna take a little trip to Fishland," he says to the women, and he hooks his arm through my arm and leads me off to the boathouse where the Lake Trout Tournament is being judged.

When we get inside, scores of people are milling around, a few women but mostly men. Half of them I take to be local farmers; the others look like they just stepped out of a sportsman's catalog—pastel-colored deck shoes, corduroy caps covered with fishing flies, vests with a hundred pockets. We get a wealthy class of tourist here in the summer. A big white-board on the wall has the weights of the largest entries listed beside the names of their conquerors. Somebody's fish is tipping the scales this very moment.

Leo shepherds me through the crowd, and who do I see at the judging stand but my own college president officiating. I don't know why I'm so surprised; the main themes of his administration are fund-raising and town-gown relations, and he fancies himself a man of the people. An attendant weighs the fish for him; it qualifies and he writes it up with a broad red marker. Then he turns around and looks right at me. His public face collapses a bit, but he comes around the table to shake our hands.

"I'm surprised to see you here, Barry," the president says, narrowing his eyes. "I'd have thought you'd be down the lake." He smiles and tries to read my father-in-law. "At the other big picnic."

"We've been fishing," Leo says. "In your tournament here."

The president widens his eyes and points to the scale.

I jump in. "We didn't catch anything," I say. "Never even had a nibble," and I'm stunned by the pain of giving this particular man that news.

"Oh, that's too bad," the president says. "Well, some

other fellows got lucky." He waves his hand at the white-board on the wall. In his mind, this encounter is over. He's already backing away.

"Those are pretty small trout for this lake, aren't they?" Leo asks. The largest fish listed is three pounds something; most of them are just over two.

The president steps back to us and becomes confidential. "We *are* seeing a smaller fish this year," he says. "We had an exceptionally hard winter, and I think it stunted their growth."

"That must be it," Leo says, and we all wave goodbye. As we leave the boathouse, Leo laughs. "He gave me his glad hand, Barry. The hand that lowers the boom."

"I've never understood how the guy got his job," I say.

"Oh, no," Leo says. "That's where you're wrong. He's perfect."

The women have assembled quite a feast for us today—lamb kabobs, potato salad, three-bean salad, strawberry pie—and now we're sitting down to it, Leo and Betty on one side of the picnic table, Beth and me on the other. Our side looks out at the lake, huge and cool and blue. The colleague who loaned me the boat calls the lake "the bil-lion-gallon pacifier" because gazing at it never fails to calm him down. A tenured man for a decade now—in Italy at the moment on a research grant—he insists that the lake has saved his mind many times in his career at this place. I could tell, in the dead of this past winter, how miserable I'd become, because I simply stopped seeing it. I'd arrive at the department and someone would say, "Wasn't the lake an incredible blue this morning?" or, "Did you see how the ice goes all the way out to the middle now?" and I'd realize that, once again, I'd walked to work in a trance—the way some people, parking their cars, cannot remember driving to wherever they are.

Beyond Leo and Betty, our town is glowing on the western bank, backlighted splendidly by the setting sun. I can tell exactly where we live by the great copper beech behind our house, one of the tallest trees in a town of strapping specimens. Its massive red-green puff towers over everything else on shore. This morning, looking out the back window next to the breakfast table, I noticed that its dark silver bark is precisely the color of Leo's hair.

For a minute I entertain the notion that my line of sight connects my spirit to the spirit of the tree, like an invisible fiber of hidden force. Then I realize where I got this idea—from the Indian maiden in the veterans' park across the street from our place. Her tribe once occupied the land we live on; this was once their lake. She's a beautiful young woman on a pedestal in a marble fountain basin, staring through the vacant lot between our house and the old Elks Club. There's a legend about her too, which says that she must always be able to see the lake; her view of the lake must never be obscured, or a terrible doom will fall upon the town. For this reason nothing can ever be built in that vacant lot. It's a law, right on the books. Fraternity boys from the college long ago broke off the maiden's nose, and every year during pledge week they spray-paint her parts. Yet there she stands staring, however desecrated and defamed.

Last fall I became concerned about the Indian maiden.

Could she still see the lake? I wondered. Had anyone bothered to check? I put on my bathing suit, walked across to the park, and waded through the fountain to stand on the pedestal behind her. I wrapped my arms around her shoulders, put my cheek to her cheek, got my eyes as close to her eyes as I could, and looked. A big green sign on the highway badly spoiled her view, not to mention the white Agway tower down by the railroad tracks. But a slender crescent of blue water was definitely visible to her. We were still all right, I thought. Still getting off on a technicality.

Now, at our picnic table, these eye-beams that hold you to your place in the world remind me of something else, and I have to laugh when I think of it—that painted fish on the billboard when you come into town, connected to a distant fisherman by a line in its mouth.

"What's so funny?" Leo says. He's pouring our white wine into plastic goblets, mock-ceremoniously.

"My kinship with a certain prizewinning fish."

"Next subject," Leo says.

The wine comes from a vineyard just down the road from here. It looks good purling from the bottle, golden and bright. We raise our disposable glasses. "To our fine family," Leo says.

"To our new granddaughter!" Betty says after him.

"To no more wars to have Memorial Days about," Beth says.

"To the great unknown," I say.

"Wait a minute," Beth says. "What's so unknown?"

I have to think of an acceptable answer. "How deep this lake is," I say at last. "Nobody knows that."

"Watch yourself, buster," she says.

"Cheers!" we all say together, and have a sip.

"This is the best one so far," Leo says. We've opened a variety of local bottles this weekend. "This one's right up there with California."

"The Chamber of Commerce would love to hear you say that," I say.

"I'm glad they're doing something right," Beth says, taking a lamb kabob and passing the platter around. "Considering what they're doing to our water."

"Your water *is* pretty awful," Betty says. "Isn't it, honey?" she asks her husband.

Leo only sighs and contemplates the contents of his glass.

"This week was particularly bad," I say.

The agricultural contamination of the lake gets especially heavy if it rains right after they've sprayed or fertilized the grapes. By Leo's standards, the equipment at our waterworks is hopelessly antique; no matter what extra pollution it senses, it simply dumps in more chlorine. Taking a bath this week has been like going to the pool at the Y, and drinking the stuff is out of the question.

I say, "Did you know there are some animals that don't need to drink water? They get all the fluid they need from the wine in their diet."

"I know one of those animals," Beth says. She lays her arm across my shoulders. "But we're removing wine from that animal's rations after this weekend. The animal's mate is giving birth, and he can't afford to be listless anymore. He has to makes lots of new pictures to get money for their nest."

When Leo and Betty leave tomorrow, I'm supposed to

start painting like a man possessed. In October, my gallery is finally giving me a one-man show. To get it, I promised entire walls of new work. But between teaching and the tenure battle and worrying about having a kid, I haven't done a single picture since last September—haven't had a picture in me to do. Three weeks ago, with the coveted summer vacation upon me at last, I began trying for real. My conclusion—Beth has heard it—is that I'll never paint again.

"The animal has made all the pictures he knows how to make," I say.

"No one believes that," Beth says. "It's in the animal's nature to do it."

"The animal has powerful enemies. Fighting them has worn him out."

"This is certainly a fascinating creature," Betty says to Leo. "What sort of animal do you suppose it is?"

"There was mention of a live birth and powerful enemies," Leo says. "I'd say it sounds like a large mammal."

Halfway through our picnic the mosquitoes arrived, rising from the grass to have dinner themselves. We gave them our ankles in return for strawberry pie at sunset, but as we ate our dessert the mosquitoes wanted theirs—ears and necks and hands—so we bolted it down and packed up our things. Now, in the beginnings of dusk, we've carried the cooler and canvas bags out to the graveled parking lot and packed them in the trunk. Beth and Betty are driving home. Leo and I have to return the borrowed boat, which we weren't supposed to keep out after dark.

I help Beth into the car; then I squat down next to the open driver's door to touch her fantastic belly. "Watch your mother's driving, Chardonnay," I say. "No tailgating, always signal before turns." And lo, Chardonnay gives my hand a little kick to signal one of her own turns in there.

"Give that child a proper name," Betty says.

"And watch your driving yourself," Beth says. "I don't like you out on the water at night."

"We'll be fine," I say, and then they're off, gravel crunching and dust flying in the headlight beams. Leo and I walk through the trees of the picnic area and onto the grassy slope that runs down to the docks. The sky is unbelievable, as it so often is. We have a full moon this evening rising into the indigo vault, Venus and a couple of stars already on view. Off to the west, an orange stroke of sunset still hangs above the town behind cloud puffs hovering like a pink-tinged balloon brigade. Halfway down the pier, we stop on the narrow strip of boards to watch it all arching over the water.

"Reminds me of one of your paintings," Leo says out of the blue.

I look at him and then I look back up in the air. It *is* a painterly sky, almost not part of life, with an otherworldly patina far beyond any mortal with a brush. Not that any of us should bother trying; only God can get away with kitsch like this.

"I'm this good, huh?"

"You're great," Leo says.

I climb down the dock ladder and into the boat, wondering if my father-in-law has me confused with Maxfield Parrish. "I don't do this kind of thing, Leo," I say, sitting behind the steering wheel.

"I didn't mean you painted this way," he says, stepping in and taking the co-pilot's seat. We have jackets in the boat, and we put them on. It's cold out here. "I meant it gives me a similar feeling."

Well, what do you know. "OK, now I'm interested," I say, and I start the boat.

He laughs and shouts above the motor. "I can't explain a feeling."

"Try."

He takes a cigar from his jacket pocket, unwraps it, and twirls it in his mouth, glancing all around himself. The moon is shining in the lake—a path of white light right down the middle as far as we can see. All we have to do is sail along this unbroken, glistening road. I hit the throttle and we glide out into it, our red and white running lights adding their trails to the moonglow in the water.

Leo looks up at the sky and chews on his cigar for half a minute, and then he shakes his head. "Well, I guess the feeling is that it's all telling some important story."

"Telling a story? That's the feeling?"

"Yeah, a story, and the point is that you have to figure out what the story is."

"So what is it?"

"I don't know," Leo says. "I haven't figured it out."

"Well, what's it about?"

"Beats me," he says.

"Hey, Leo," I say. "You're talking to a desperate man here. Don't string me along. You started this. Figure it out and tell me what it is."

Now I've startled him, but that's the way it has to be. He looks at the horizon again and then up at the sky, breathing very deeply. "Is it OK if it sounds stupid?" he says.

"That's probably the only thing that would be OK."

"OK," he says. "The glory of it all."

"The glory of it all?" I start to laugh. "That's the story? That's what it's about?"

"Yeah. I'm sorry, Barry. I don't know anything about art."

I begin to howl. I pound the steering wheel with the heel of my hand. Then I grab Leo's chin and kiss his stubbly cheek.

His smile comes back, but he's giving that poor cigar a real beating. "Did I say something right?" he says.

"I don't know, Leo. It's just a feeling. I can't explain it." And then I crack up again and push the throttle all the way, and we hurtle down the lake.

Between the moon itself and its reflection in the water, we're sailing inside a spooky abundance of light—more light than there should be at night, enough light to see that the high chain-link fence of the army depot has already begun, running in front of the trees on the eastern bank to our left. The lake boundary of the depot extends south for miles from here; my colleague who owns the boat lives across the water from the place, and he worries about it. He thinks the Russians might drop their first one right here, and he might be right about that. I point it out to Leo. "See the watchtowers?" I shout above our motor, showing him their silhouettes above the trees.

He looks at them and nods. Then he says, "I want you to

forget what I said before about guarantees. I think you should fight this college, and I'll tell you why."

But just as he begins, the bright path of moonlight vanishes from the lake and we can't even see each other. The moon itself is gone from the sky, only a vague glow remaining where it used to be. I'm steering us into blackness. I shut down our motor and its noise seems not to stop but to leap out of the boat and up over our heads, as if the motor's soul has flown away to rumble in the sky.

Then the moon slides back into place, and we see the enormous black airplane coming down right on top of us. It takes up half the sky and makes me sick to see the size of it. We cower in our seats, hands over heads, eyes riveted on the horrible plane. Moonlight hits its wings as it descends, and we see that it's not black at all but camouflage-painted, and as gruesome as a thing could be. We hear its behemoth roar, watch the four huge propellers gnashing in its front like maws.

It passes through the air like a monster from a dream; then it disappears behind the trees around the depot. For a minute we sit stunned in the bobbing boat, gripping the hull and breathing like frightened animals. I can tell exactly the size and shape of my heart, it's slamming so hard. My arms and legs are actually shaking. And I remember now what I heard at the protest rally last year—that the depot conceals its real business by flying the missiles in and out in secret, only at night, in mammoth cargo transports with no landing lights.

Leo says a couple of curses I didn't even know he knew, and I say a couple too. After a few minutes we calm down and start to laugh about it. And then I look over at the shore and nearly fall overboard. Five or six dead-white faces are staring out at us from behind the depot fence. It takes me a few seconds to figure out what they are, the only thing they could possibly be.

"Look, Leo," I say, pointing them out. "Ghosts."

He looks, and sees them, and gasps. I start the boat and move us as quietly as I can in their direction. They don't seem to mind our approach, but twenty yards out I shut the motor down again. I don't know this bank of the lake at all, don't dare come in any closer at night. And this is close enough. Leo sees they're not ghosts, and he punches me in the shoulder for scaring him.

They're deer, a whole half dozen of the famous snow-white deer that live inside the army depot. They say you can only see them at dawn or dusk; I've been hoping for a glimpse ever since moving here. Their ancestors were common brown whitetails trapped inside decades ago when the army sealed off these thousands of acres with a fence too high for deer to jump. Since then, they've lived and bred as an island population, and now—countless deer generations later—they're born without any coloring at all. These six are standing in a huddle staring at us, heads almost touching, noses pressed to the fence, every one of them like a cloud in the shape of a deer. I think of the Indian maiden and wonder what she and her tribe would make of these blank, spectral beasts—if they would think of them as spirits of the original creatures sealed inside so long ago. In a way, I think, that's what they are.

And the instant I think that, my new painting comes to me. It simply appears and I see it, exactly the way it's going to be.

It's a painting of the unfathomable lake. The sweeping blue is sometimes simply water, cold and deep. But at other places in the painting it's not water at all. It's more like a condition, a blue situation that other things are in. It's daytime in some parts of this painting; in other parts it's night. A gorgeous sunset is happening above the town— quite Maxfield Parrish-ish, in fact, with those fiery clouds— but a full moon and stars are out, too, and the sun is shining besides. The terrible black plane is coming in for a landing, missiles tumbling from its belly into the lake where fish are leaping to bite colorful lures that fly above the water like songbirds, shreds of milfoil dangling from their hooks. The Indian maiden appears as a statue at the wheel of a powerboat, eye-beams from her face shining on the slick dark head of a monster rising from the blue. But across the canvas she appears again—a living woman on the shore near a gigantic red-green copper beech. The living princess and members of her tribe are feeding wine grapes to snow-white deer who eat the fruit and then float away as clouds to take their place inside the sunset. An angel with hair precisely the color of the beech tree's bark is hovering above the lake, casting a spell on the water to make it pure. And in the shade of the great tree, watched over by tribespeople and deer, a man and a woman have just had a baby, a little girl they've wanted all their lives. They hold her up like a story they've finally been able to tell, naked and red against the lake and sky, and they give her the name Glory.

JAZZERS

Some *outrageous music is* playing on the sound system in this place—clearly the bartender has brought along his own favorite albums tonight. This one is by a hot electric quartet doing jazz standards and some original tunes, everything with a great cool feel and hip harmonies. All the players are wonderful, but the guitarist is a monster. It sounds like his fingers are connected directly to his ears. He doesn't so much play as *sing*. There's a lot of rock in his jazz, a lot of blues in his rock, and the most thrilling, punchy sound coming out of his amp. He's playing the guitar exactly the way I've always wanted to play it. I don't know how I've missed this guy—another incredible guitar player from out of nowhere. You close your eyes for five minutes and everything changes.

Five minutes ago Bobby began to cry and went to the men's room so I wouldn't see him doing it. Now he's just sniffling and blinking his eyes, holding on to his beer and looking down at the table. When we came in, I took a booth in the back thinking this place would be swarming after a while; so far, it's still only the two of us and the bartender. The privacy would be torture without this music to escape into.

Bobby looks up at me and tries to smile. "Isn't this some shit," he says.

For a second I think he means the music, but he's still talking about Chris, his wife. I told Bobby everything I could tell him when he called on the phone, told him he already had plenty of skills as a victim without any help from me. Then I felt bad and agreed to come out and meet him. When I got here I told him the same things again anyway.

"This is the real shit right here," I say to him now, waving my hand at the speakers hanging from the ceiling. "Are you checking this out? When did you ever hear 'Stella by Starlight' like this?" I mimic the guitar player with my fingers. "Burning, man."

Bobby and I used to do "Stella" together. Everybody does "Stella."

"Burning," he says, swirling his beer, watching it spin around and fizz.

They've just remodeled and reopened this place and spent a lot of money doing it. I'd like to come back here soon, bring Janet and some other friends, have a good time in a nice bar with great music. But I wonder if this neighborhood can sustain a place like this. I was in here once, before it changed hands, when there was a depressing jukebox full of oldies and a bunch of old regulars at the rail.

Now it has track lighting on a flat-black ceiling, *faux* marble columns painted on the walls, wild artwork hanging all over the place. The new proprietors must think they're in New York City instead of Baltimore. I can't remember what this bar used to be called, but it's called All Out now. I'm staring at red-and-blue neon tubes in the front window announcing the new name to a dark, empty street.

The band on the record finishes the wonderful "Stella" they've been doing, and in the silence between tracks I glance over at the bartender. He's loping around behind the bar, wiping glasses, hanging them by their stems from the new wooden rack above his head. The next tune comes on, and he bops his head in time with it. It's "The Night Has a Thousand Eyes."

Bobby has flattened his beer by swirling it around. I thought I'd be carrying him out of here tonight, but he's not interested in drinking. "I'd like to know what I'm supposed to do," he says to me now.

I feel for Bobby, I really do, but I can't go into that. I've lost count of the times I've seen him in shreds on account of his wife. Now he wants me to help him run himself through the meat slicer a few more times. He knows what to do.

"I think we should start playing again, Bobby," I say. "I think it was a mistake to let the music slide."

"Oh, man," he says, and he lets his head bang against the wall of our booth.

We used to play in a band—Bobby on keyboards, me on guitar—with a sax player, bass player, and drummer he knew. We did standards and some newer things, only good tunes, all with jazzy idealism and no concessions to the marketplace. We worked our day jobs, played nights and weekends. Some cafés and lounges used us for six months or so, but we didn't attract a following and the work dried up. We were just starting to sound good. We kept rehearsing for a while, and then I stopped seeing Bobby. That was almost a year ago. He's in computer-programming school now. Chris talked him into doing it. He borrowed the money from his folks.

"Next round's on me," I say, sliding out of the booth. Bobby insisted on paying for the first drinks we had, even though he has, I think, all of ten bucks to walk around with. "You want something to eat? Maybe they've got the grill going. My treat. Pretzels, at least."

He shakes his head, ears sticking out. This afternoon he had his black hair chopped off to about two inches all around. It used to be shoulder-length and fluffy.

The bartender is a tall, rangy guy with long brown hair parted in the middle, plaid flannel shirt, a satisfied expression on his face. He's maybe all of twenty-two, and he doesn't look like he comes from around here. He looks like Colorado or New Mexico, somewhere like that. He's snapping his fingers and swinging his arms as I walk up to the bar. He smiles at me, big white teeth. Two gold stud earrings are in his left ear, one in his right.

I smile back. "Great music," I say, pointing to the CD machine behind the bar. At this moment, the bass player is taking a mean solo over some airy chord changes the guitarist is flinging at him.

The bartender nods and lifts his eyebrows and holds up a finger for me to wait. Then he rummages among cassettes and compact discs and hands me the plastic case for the CD he's playing.

"The grill working?" I ask.

"Next week for the grill," he says. "Place just opened, the grill isn't together yet."

"Then let me have two more drafts and some pretzels."

"No pretzels," he says. "Pretzel distributor didn't come through." He rattles the empty pretzel rack. "It's just popcorn tonight," he says. "Homemade, all you want on the house."

"I meant popcorn," I say.

He draws the beer, and I look at the album's liner notes. I've never heard of a single person in this band, and the guitar player is a woman. "I give up," I say, shaking my head and waving the paper insert. "There's too much going on."

The bartender laughs and pushes the glasses across the bar. Then he fetches a few more CDs and hands them to me. "Here's some more to worry about," he says. He scoops a wicker basket full of popcorn from a big plastic garbage bag beneath the shelf of liquor bottles and sets the basket on the glasses of beer. The other albums feature the same musicians. I copy the titles onto a bar napkin while he rings up the drinks.

"You play?" he asks when he hands me my change. I hand him back a dollar bill, and he winks and puts it in the pocket of his shirt.

"Guitar," I say.

"Hey," he says. "Like this?" He points up at the music in the air.

"Like this but not this good." I laugh.

He laughs too, and nods, tapping the woman's picture on one of the discs. "She's too much, isn't she?" he says.

We shake hands and tell each other our names. His is Carl. He plays tenor and soprano sax. He's from Kansas, just moved here to help his friends open this bar.

"My friend plays keyboards," I say, and I nod my head toward Bobby, who's slumped down in the booth staring at the door to the ladies' room in back. "We had a combo for a while, just a lounge thing. He's having some troubles tonight. Woman troubles."

Carl raises his hands as if in surrender. "Say no more," he says. Then he says that he might be free to do some jamming in a week or two, and we trade phone numbers on bar napkins for that.

"Maybe my friend too," I say.

"Sure," Carl says.

And then five people walk in the door all at once—two men, three women, very talky and happy—and take the front table beneath the window. The women sit down in the red-and-blue glow of the neon sign. Carl promises to play the other albums and walks down the bar to take the order from the two men. On my way back to our booth, the popcorn basket balanced on the glasses, I smile and nod hello to the women, and they smile and nod back. I can tell which one is unattached. She's thin and blond and very pretty.

Bobby has become a different man in the five minutes I've been at the bar. He's stoic now, not asking for comfort or advice. He just wants a place to stay for the night; he's not going home. He takes a pack of cigarettes out of his jacket, lights one, blows the smoke up over my head. He'd been restraining himself.

"You quit," I remind him.

"I started again," he says.

I light one of the cigarettes too, probably the first I've had since I stopped playing music with Bobby a year ago. It tastes like they did when I was fifteen years old, and I think for a minute about being that age. When cigarettes tasted as alien as this, I was taking guitar lessons in a music store, playing in bands with friends after school, wearing the grooves off records trying to figure out how my heroes did what they did. My teacher was a purist jazzer named Eddie who closed his eyes and drifted away when he played, snapped his fingers when he wasn't playing, wore shades and a black beret. He made a big impression on us with his beatnik act, all us little jazzlings showing up like altar boys once a week with our guitars.

Except that it wasn't an act. Bebop was the world for Eddie, and it pained him greatly that I also dug Clapton and Hendrix and the Beatles. Jazz was a kind of life, Eddie would say, a life based on a kind of music. That life didn't have anything to do with having spangles on your clothes or being on TV or jumping up and down on a stage. I had to try to understand that, he would say. I remember now that Eddie could be a frightening guy sometimes. I was just a kid who thought that if you could reach people with an electric guitar, you were king of the world.

Behind the bar, Carl is putting another CD in the machine. He holds the cover up so I can see which one it is.

"Carl over there plays sax," I tell Bobby. "He'd be into jamming sometime soon."

Bobby turns his cigarette around, examining it. "All God's chillun are into jamming sometime soon," he says.

"All got soul." He flicks a piece of popcorn against the wall and watches it bounce back across the table. Then he smirks and takes a drag on the cigarette and leaves it hanging from his lips. When he speaks, it bounces in the corner of his mouth like a conductor's baton. "All God's crappy chillun are jammers and artistes," he says, smoke spilling out of his nose.

The guy Bobby's wife is sleeping with is a painter. She bought one of his paintings at a show; that's how they met. This morning Bobby pulled the painting off the wall and threw it out their fourth-floor window onto the street. Chris went out to get it, and she didn't come back.

The other album comes on, funkier than the first and louder—Carl has jacked up the volume a good bit. The woman on guitar is now playing screaming rock licks through a wah-wah pedal. Halfway through the first cut, the people sitting by the window get up and start dancing in the space between the bar and the tables. Carl approves. He's biting his lower lip and snapping his fingers, doing a funny imitation of ecstasy.

"Invasion of the body snatchers," Bobby says. He wants to use the bathroom and leave, and as he's sliding out of his seat, the blond woman dances between the tables toward our booth and asks with her hands if we want to join in.

"Go ahead," Bobby says. "Dance a dance. I can wait."

I smile at her and shake my head. She makes a pouting face and shrugs and dances back. Carl has a saxophone strap around his neck, and he's pulling a shiny golden tenor from a case propped open on the bar.

.   .   .

Janet has heard the latest installment of the Bobby saga. I told her after he called. She's down on Bobby and didn't want me coming out here to meet him. She said people like Bobby always take advantage of me. She had a long list of examples. I don't want to bring him home without letting her know. The pay phone is back in the corridor with the rest rooms, and while I'm fooling with my coins I can hear Bobby scat-singing behind the men's room door.

My number is busy. Back at the booth I put on my jacket, light another one of Bobby's cigarettes, sip some of the rest of my beer. Carl is rambling around behind the bar, blowing his tenor to the record while the people dance. The blond-haired woman is clapping her hands and cheering him on. He plays very good sax. Bobby comes back, and when we get up to the bar I shout to Carl that I'll call him in a week. He takes a hand off the horn to wave goodbye.

Out on the street the quiet is almost funny, nestled up against the loud music and dancing on the other side of the door. There's no traffic at all, nothing happening except three guys standing on the corner waiting for something. I don't see how this bar can make it in this neighborhood.

Bobby hasn't come out of the place. Through the window I see him laughing with Carl, writing something on a napkin, paying Carl for a package. When he comes out, he holds it up.

"A six-pack for the road," he says. "The long road."

"You didn't have to do that," I say. "I have some beer at home."

When we get to my car, he puts a quarter in the parking meter and turns the crank.

"What did you do that for?"

"They sell time out here," he says. "I bought you some."

When we get rolling, he twists open a bottle and starts drinking.

"Suddenly you like beer," I say. "We're in a bar, perfectly nice bar, all the beer in the world, perfectly good beer, great music, people dancing, having a good time, you have to leave. In the car you like to drink. It's illegal to drink in the car."

"Bobby's a problem," he says. He takes another swallow from the bottle, then he turns on the radio and makes like he's dancing in his seat. "So why didn't you dance with the blond one?" he says. "I saw you checking her out. Nice. Surfboards, bikinis, coral reefs. You could have danced with her, made her feel accepted and worthwhile. She wanted you to do that for her, man, but you turned her down. Tsk, tsk."

"She asked both of us. You didn't dance with her either."

"Yeah, but I wasn't flirting with her. I got a wife to be faithful to, pal," he says, and he laughs this sick laugh. Then he says, "Well, you talked me into it."

"Talked you into what?"

"Into playing music. I'm ready to play. Tonight, right now. And don't say it's too late."

"It's too late. Janet'll be in bed, and we can't make any noise. I have to get up in the morning and go to work."

"I didn't say I wanted to play at your place. You can't go in tomorrow and rustle those papers if you miss a little sleep?"

"I thought you didn't want to go home."

"Not home. I know some cats across town. They're always jamming."

I'm zipping along in third all the way up St. Paul, the lights turning green like a string of necklace beads, like they see me coming. We're home, like that. "What cats?" I say.

"Some cats, never mind. I'm going there to play. I don't have a car, so you have to take me. You might as well bring your gee-tar."

"I don't know, Bobby," I say, pulling the hand brake and switching the headlights off.

"You know," he says, and gets out.

Upstairs, Bobby falls on the sofa and lights a cigarette. Janet is awake in bed, reading a magazine. I close the bedroom door. "He needs a place to stay," I say.

She's annoyed, staring past her hands, not saying anything.

"We're gonna go play some music with some guys he knows. Just for a couple of hours." She gives me a disgusted look. I sit down on the bed and rub her knees through the blanket. "I tried to call. The line was busy."

"I was on for a while," she says, moving her legs away. "You smell like smoke."

I get up, find some guitar picks and put them in my pocket, coil an electric guitar cord around my hand. "Who were you talking to?"

"Steve called."

"Steve," I say. I look around for my guitar. She's put it somewhere. "What's on Steve's mind?"

"He's in town tomorrow on business. He wants to take me out to dinner."

"Take you out to dinner. Like the last time."

"No, not like the last time. He knows we're together and it's just dinner. Don't start."

"We were together the last time, and it was just dinner then too."

"We weren't together the way we're together now. Steve knows what's what. I'm going out to dinner with him. Period. Go play your guitar."

"If I could find it, I would."

"I put it in the hall closet. I kept tripping over it where it was."

My guitar's in the closet, upside down. In the living room, Bobby seems to be sleeping on the sofa. I drag my amplifier out of the corner and set it next to the door. He opens his eyes and smiles.

"Hey, soul train," he says. "Ready to roll into jazzland?"

In the car, Bobby sings and drums out rhythms on his knees, a beer bottle sticking up from between his legs. He's making fun of the blues. "Oh, my baby," he sings in a raspy voice, "she done gone and done me wrong. Ooh hoo." Then he sings a trumpet lick to fill in behind that, mimicking a trumpet player with his hands. He looks happy, drinking and giving me directions to some place all the way over on the east side of town. I'm drinking a beer too, holding it in my lap while I drive. Bobby lights a cigarette and feels his flattened pack. He waves the pack in the air.

"I see a place coming up," he says. Then he swings his empty bottle by its throat. "We could get some more of these bad boys, too."

I park near a small storefront lit up with five or six neon beer signs. Inside, they have a bulletproof Plexiglas barrier separating the customers from the clerk and the merchandise, with a revolving Plexiglas drum for exchanging the money and goods. It feels like being inside a huge pinball machine. I don't know how much further things can go here in Baltimore. Maybe next they'll start selling booze and cigarettes from armored tanks parked in the street. Three expensive beer clocks are flashing three wildly different times above some old folks lined up to play a row of video poker games and be somewhere warm. On our way out of the store, a tall, skinny black kid goes in past us with a naked electric bass slung over his shoulder—just the bass, no case, and it's wintertime.

"Musicians," I say to Bobby. "They're dropping out of the sky."

"You think he's any good?" Bobby says. "I bet he's incredible. And you'll never hear him. You'll never see him again. The world wipes its butt with incredible bass players."

On the sidewalk, an old woman in a print dress steps out of a doorway to ask for spare change. I give her what's in my pocket, thirty-five cents. Bobby rummages in his coat and then hands her several one-dollar bills. She looks at her hand like it's not really connected to her. Bobby pats her shoulder, and she hustles right into the store. "Gas money," he says to me and laughs. "I don't need it, and she gets terrible mileage."

Bobby's wife took their car when she left with the painting. It's her car. Bobby never did have a car of his own, and his motorcycle is broken the way it always was.

"You been playing?" he asks when we get rolling again.

"I've been practicing at home," I say. "Learning a few tunes."

"Not getting out with anybody?"

"Nobody I know needs a guitar player for gigs, and nobody wants to play just for the sake of playing. The telephone has to sound like it has money in it or people won't even pick it up when it rings. I work, I'm tired. Haven't met anybody new."

"You'll meet these people tonight. I've played over here a few times."

"Really."

"Yeah, you know, hitch a ride over, sit in for a few tunes. I met one of these guys in a club."

"I'm into playing," I say.

"I always thought you could have been a real good guitar player," he says. "I never understood what was keeping you from it. I think you have trouble with long-term commitments." He burps and then he starts to laugh. It starts out as sad, painful laughter, but then it becomes the real thing, and it makes me start laughing too, and in this way we proceed across town in my car, two men seized by a fit of pointless joy.

Soon we're in a neighborhood where half the buildings have been boarded up and spray-painted with graffiti. It looks like World War Three out here. Bobby shows me where to park, and we unload my stuff. He rings a bell on a big brownstone. His friends are jamming, all right—even on the sidewalk you can hear this hard Latin bop happening up there. Nobody answers the bell. We try the street door and find it unlocked. In the dark stairwell the music is like a rocket taking off. We're almost disembodied by the volume of it, my equipment seeming to haul us up the stairs. On the third floor I can't even hear Bobby banging on the door. He laughs and pushes it open.

Inside, four or five people are wailing away in a front parlor room full of drums and instruments and amplifiers. A young Asian woman in the kitchen down at the end of the hall sees us and comes out, realizes it's Bobby, grabs his head, and runs her hands all over his skull, amazed by what he's done to his hair. But she likes it. She kisses him on both cheeks and smiles at me, and Bobby introduces us by screaming into our ears. Her name is Tamara. Bobby sits down on my amp, offers Tamara one of our beers, hands me one and a cigarette. I can see the bass player and drummer laying down the groove in the corner. They don't have a guitar player. There's a hypnotic painting hanging on one wall that looks like a computer chip or somebody's chromosomes. On another wall there's a portrait of John Coltrane —a wild version of his famous profile from *A Love Supreme*, with splashes of colors painted all around his head.

They've been playing "All the Things You Are." When they finish the tune, the keyboard player stands up so Bobby can sit in. "Check out the dude's hair!" he says, and then everybody else sees Bobby and they make a great commotion about his transformed head. He just laughs and runs his hands across the keys to warm himself up, sounding every bit as good as the other guy. The sax player sees me strapping on my guitar and looking at Coltrane on the wall, and he decides we should play "Impressions"—probably the most common Coltrane tune there is, but I forget how it goes. Bobby perceives this. "D minor," he says to me. "Then E flat, then back down to D again. Easiest thing in the world." He smiles, and the band starts to play.

I listen for a minute, feeling what I hear, trying to get a message from the realm of D minor. That was what Eddie told me to do when I took lessons with him. I think that D minor signifies such and such, and I touch the guitar, and the chord that comes out sounds like the moon appearing from behind a cloud. I touch it again, and the same thing happens. Everything I do sounds delightful. Ideas that seemed stale and aimless at home are fresh and solid with other people playing. I'm surprised I managed to forget that. It's such a succulent sensation, putting your sound in with other people's sounds. When it's time for me to solo, I hear myself playing before I can even worry about what to play.

We do a couple of other tunes. If I don't know the tune we're doing, I play what I can from the chart. If I can't play anything, I don't try. Eddie taught me that too. He really knew what this was all about, the disaffected, moody bebopper.

Somewhere between tunes we say our names and shake hands. Tony, Ricardo, Cecil, Doug, Misaki. Bobby and me. Tamara has been in an easy chair applauding enthusiastically after every song. "Like Jell-O," she says. "Like a room of Jell-O. With Cool Whip."

"Tamara digs Jell-O," Bobby explains to me. "She was

telling me another time I was here. It's like a symbol or something."

Tamara just laughs. She's the painter of the work hanging in the room. More of her pictures are up all around the apartment—wild, throbbing things like bruises ripening on the walls. "Play another song," she says.

We do that. The bursts of music detach themselves from us and float out among Tamara's paintings like bubbles we're blowing. Bobby in particular sounds amazing tonight. His playing hits me as a series of excavations of himself, one layer after another revealed by the notes. We're doing a bouncy but mysterious "Windows," and in Bobby's long solo I think I hear the agony of marriage to Chris, the many years of not knowing what to do next, the broken motorcycle against the wall in his living room, the arc of his rival's painting sailing out the window and over the street. I hear him tossing computer school out the window too, tossing just about everything. Eventually his solo feathers away, and he sits up straight at the keyboard, looking at me.

I begin to think about what the opening chord of "Windows" might mean (it's B♭ minor⁷), when suddenly the nature of chords doesn't interest me anymore. It's suddenly more interesting to think about Steve wrecking his expensive car on the way to pick Janet up for dinner, and I hear myself playing that, playing Steve trudging back to his hotel with a steering wheel in his hand, the seat ripped out of his tailored pants. Then I make a big motorcycle appear. It's Bobby with Chris on the back. They've kissed and made up and finally fixed his broken bike, and now as he pulls up onto the sidewalk, Chris whacks Steve over the head with her ex-lover's oil painting. Then she and Bobby zoom away, cackling into the night. Bobby's synthesizer is sticking up out of the sidecar attached to the bike because they're on their way to his first gig with our new band. At the gig, the whole world is in the audience and we sound great. It's especially nice to see old Eddie out there, still in his black beret, still sipping dark ale and smoking Pall Malls. He gives me the OK sign. And then, in the middle of our set, Janet and Chris get up on stage behind the band and begin to unfurl large banners they've painted as a surprise for us. DON'T THEY SOUND GREAT? the first banner says. THE JAZZ LIFE! The audience applauds. THEY'RE GOOD MEN! the second banner says, with arrows pointing to Bobby and me. THERE'S NOTHING WRONG WITH THEM! WE REALIZE THAT NOW! Great cheering erupts out there among the masses. Then the women unfurl the third banner. HOW COULD WE EVER HAVE WANTED ANYONE ELSE? WHAT WERE WE THINKING? WE'RE SORRY! This one brings the crowd to its feet. Bobby beams at me from the keyboard. We're happy men at last. We only wish the skinny bass player from the liquor store could have joined our group too. But instead of being used to wipe the butt of the world, he's just been elected President of the United States. On the front page of the *Times* this morning we saw a picture of Buster (that's his name), sitting on his desk in the Oval Office, slapping out some riffs on his ax. . . .

And that's the end of my solo, all I wanted to say. I hope it sounded good. I had a fine time playing it. I look up from the guitar, and I see Carl the bartender standing across the room by the door, still in his coat, bopping his head and flashing his teeth at me. The blond woman from the bar is standing next to him. Her friends are here too, carrying six-packs and the garbage bag full of popcorn. Carl pulls out his sax, and then he prances over with the horn in his mouth and starts lovingly coming on to everybody in the room, to Tamara's paintings, to the room itself, to Chick Corea for writing the tune, to the entire darkened city.

Bobby wouldn't quit playing after everybody else called it a night. In the end, Tamara dragged him off the synthesizer and made him have something to eat. The man hadn't eaten a thing all day. Then he cracked all of us up, dancing and carrying on. I finally got him to leave by claiming to have powerful drugs down in the car. He conked out on the way home, and now getting him up the stairs is a major ordeal.

In my living room he plops onto the sofa again and lights a cigarette. He lies there with his eyes closed, smoking and flicking his ashes into the fireplace that doesn't work.

I walk through the bedroom into the bathroom. When I come out, the flushing toilet has woken Janet up.

"What time is it?" she says. "What are you doing? Come to bed."

"I'll be there in a minute," I say.

I get a couple of beers from the refrigerator. Bobby has rolled over on the sofa and buried his face in the cushions, the short black tufts of his new haircut pointing in all directions. His head looks like a little kid's head. His cigarette is lying on the oak floor Janet and I sanded and polyurethaned, and when I pick it up there's a mark like a black finger in the wood. It's four in the morning. What I most want to do this moment is play the guitar again. Certain thrilling notions are running through my hands; they might never come back, but the world won't tolerate music right now.

"Hey, Bobby," I say. I nudge him in the shoulder. "You sounded great tonight, Bobby. Really great."

He doesn't move. I lean over him with a beer bottle and twist off the cap right next to his ear. He just lies there.

"Bobby, let's put together another band," I say. "With these guys tonight or some other guys. And do regular gigs out in clubs again. You know this is what we should be doing. It's not too late to do it."

He doesn't budge, but I know he can hear me. So I tell him what was coming to me when I was playing tonight. I go into all the details, and it takes me a while. I help myself to his cigarettes. I finish my beer and start on his. I tell Bobby how exciting it was when I jumped right out of myself and into the music—how I was actually somewhere else, not in that room at all. I tell him that all anybody ever has to do is stay excited.

"Bobby, do you follow what I'm saying? I'm talking about you, man. I'm saying that everything's gonna work out. Your problems are over, Bobby. It came to me in a vision."

He shudders and stretches finally, and then he rolls in one motion on the sofa until he's facing me. His eyes don't open but his mouth does. "Incredible, man," he says. "Terrific." Then he puts one hand over his closed eyes and points the other hand at the ceiling. "Could you kill that light?" he says. "I'm sleeping."

JUNGLE VIDEO

Last night, the neighborhood skunks invaded my dreams. They emerged from the dumpster at the restaurant where I used to work and followed me to my old apartment building—a black-and-white throng nipping at my heels. Their pointy faces snuffled my shoes as my ex-girlfriend said that she wasn't alone and I couldn't come in. Then the skunks wiggled with me down endless lonely streets to a sound track of electric guitars, garbage cans tumbling over, and a peculiar popping noise that turned out to be people trading small-weapons fire from the rooftops. And just now, when crashing sounds from upstairs woke me, it all made more sense than you want your dreams to make: in the full light of morning my bedroom reeks of skunk. The little beasts must have been rooting outside the house all night.

I wrap a pillow around my head but it only amplifies the commotion above me. A man of average stature and need for rest, I live below the workplace of insomniac giants. Anita is six feet three, Dwight several inches taller. Their footfalls boom in the ceiling. Now they're knocking things over and screaming at each other.

I shuffle out to the kitchen in my robe. Someone has been down to make coffee. I pour myself a mug of it and head upstairs. All the second-floor offices are empty, so I push open the door to the big editing suite. The only light comes from the shimmering television screens and the tall racks of video decks and special-effects generators blinking against the wall: the hidden engines of Paradise Productions humming away in an old house on a working-class street in Boston. Nobody's here, either. The sounds are coming from the large attic-floor office overhead. I punch that intercom number on the telephone. The pandemonium stops and someone scrambles to answer. It's Dwight. "Why, Walter," he says. "How nice to hear your voice. Where are you?" Then I hear a loud grunt and the sound of the phone clattering to the floor.

After a minute Dwight gets on again. "Anita just tackled me," he says. "It's not a good time to talk. We're wrestling."

"It sounded like you were here in the editing room, right on top of my bed."

"We started down there."

"You wrestled up the stairs?"

"Yeah. Can I call you back? I'm in a half nelson right now." He hangs up, and the crashing and screaming begin again.

I look at the pictures flickering on the three color TVs above the editing table—faces and scenery we've been staring at all week, trying to get the first cut of a marketing tape ready for a big software outfit out on Route 128. A bowl of popcorn is on the video controller console, and stray kernels lead to the hot-air popper sitting on a stack of tape cassettes. As soon as I see it, I remember the racket it makes—a sound very much like small-weapons fire. At the other end of the table, our script is glowing on Anita's computer screen. I scroll through, up and down, and I find long passages of voice-over narration I've never seen. Sound bites we'd rejected long ago are back, whole sequences are moved to places we'd agreed were wrong, and most of the stuff I wrote is simply gone. All this since midnight, when I stumbled downstairs like a zombie.

They're playing music above me now and throwing each other against the walls. I head back down to take a shower and shave. Even the bathroom—its one window sealed shut behind the shower curtain—smells of skunk.

Nobody knows why the skunk population exploded this year, but they've taken over this neighborhood. I was walking down to the corner store one night in early spring when I saw my first gang of them, four bad customers staking out a nearby yard. Coming home with my six-pack, I found three more at the curb, heads poked through holes in a garbage bag. They looked up when they heard me coming, lettuce shreds dangling from their lips, and stared me down until I crossed the street. Then they went back to eating. Since then, I've seen skunks every night, scores of them traipsing through yards and working the gutters. We have our own family of four or five residing in tunnels beneath the unpruned shrubs; at twilight you can lean over the porch railing and watch them surface into our scrap of front lawn. We tell ourselves there's something wonderful about it—the natural world reasserting itself in the urban landscape.

I get dressed and go back upstairs. When I reach the attic office, Anita and Dwight are lying beneath an afghan on the pulled-out sofa bed, their clothes in a heap on the floor. They wave to me. "You really have to meet my friend Rebecca," Anita says.

I pretend not to know what she's talking about. She's been saying this for months, and so far she has failed to produce any such woman. She turns to Dwight. "I want Walter to meet Rebecca."

"Just say yes," Dwight says to me.

"Don't you people ever sleep?" I say. "Didn't you go home at all? I heard popcorn popping in the dead of night."

"We might catch a few winks right now," Dwight says.

"Now? Dwight, the client is coming here at three o'clock."

"Oh, we're in good shape with that," Anita says.

"We are?"

When I left last night she called it a terrible crisis.

"Sure, we're fine. After you went to bed, the Doctor showed up, and we all got this huge burst of energy and just started ripping it apart. You should have been there. We put on music and made popcorn and got some really neat ideas. We changed everything all around. Wait till you see it."

Dwight yawns. "Actually," he says, "we still don't have that elusive thing they call the vision."

"That's true," Anita says. "But this is just the rough cut."

"Anita," I say. "We've been agreeing all week that it was working. We agreed it was fine."

She smiles, sticks her foot out from under the afghan, and pats me on the knee with her toes. "I did agree to those things," she says. "It makes you so sad when I don't."

Anita and Dwight and the Doctor went into business for themselves because they couldn't work for other people anymore. True, a number of people couldn't work with them anymore either, but that was just as well. They always had more offers than they could possibly take. They're practically famous. You've seen documentaries they've produced, news programs they've directed, public-affairs specials they've researched and written. But they always had to work when other people wanted them to work, and do what other people told them to do. After a number of years they wearied of it. And then, overnight, everybody needed a video to announce his or her essence to the world, and Anita and Dwight and the Doctor became a corporation.

Six months ago, on the darkest day of winter, I sublet the first floor from them, agreeing to share the kitchen and bath. For three years, I'd been living with Jeanette, across the river in Cambridge, waiting on tables and acting in any play I could find. Then Jeanette dug up a young law partner to take my place. She'd been unhappy from the beginning, she said, and that rocked me: next to her I couldn't act at all. After I moved here, I saw the video folks every day as they rambled through my apartment to get coffee or use the john. "Forget that woman, Walter," Anita would say whenever she drifted in or out. It became an incantation, and after a while it began to work. I did begin to forget. If I started to remember, I hung around with the busy, happy people upstairs. One night, while they screened some footage, Anita discovered that I could pick shots and write a script and do it for not much money. I've been in corporate video ever since.

When I left Anita and Dwight on the sofa bed, I went down to watch the new version of our tape. Anita is a visual person. With the help of her partners, she'd snipped all the logical threads we'd spent a week spinning out, and now we had twenty minutes of pictorial free association, cut to the music I heard in my dream. I made believe I was the client and asked myself what I thought. "Are you people out of your minds?" I replied.

Now we're in the editing room, and Anita is talking to the television. "Steady up, Doctor," she says, twisting a knob to make the tape go forward and back, looking for a decent place to cut into the shot. "Steady up, goddammit."

The Doctor himself shot the footage we're looking at right now. We call him the Doctor because he has a Harvard Ph.D.—anthropology: kinship patterns of cannibals or something. He's actually a decent amateur cameraman, but this is wobbling all over the place and going in and out of focus. It's a shot of many people sitting in an enormous room, busily using computers in a way that suggests roaring productivity and satisfaction. Happiness, even. We need a shot like this, Anita says, and she's right. We need it because our client's last software release contained enough horrific bugs to corrupt databases all across the country. Heads rolled, we gather, at their new building on 128. But now it's all fixed, they claim, and that's why we're making this tape. In a few weeks they're bringing their biggest customers to town for a gala product unveiling in a fancy hotel, where they'll feature the premiere of our video on a giant screen. So yes, of course, we need a shot like this. And we have plenty of them. Would Anita produce this assignment and not bring home a bucketful of such shots? But today she doesn't like them anymore. The light is wrong, or the angle is, or the people don't look excited enough. Something invisible to me bothers Anita about every one of the happy-user shots we already have.

Instead she wants to use this one the Doctor took last week in Harvard Square while he was wandering around with the hand-held camera. He ended up in a vast basement at his alma mater where students were testing a new system to make computers do their homework.

I tell Anita, "This footage has nothing to do with our client's business or products. Using it would be misleading and unethical. It would be pure video trickery. We cannot use this shot, Anita, and you know it."

"I like the way it looks," she tells me. And then she says, "Now if only we had that perfect testimonial from a satisfied purchasing agent."

I turn my head to the wall and pretend to be deaf. Earlier this week, she got the idea of shooting me as this hypothetical purchasing person. Working me in as an actor is one of Anita's themes, like fixing me up with her friend.

The intercom buzzes. It's Dwight. He wants me to come

upstairs and talk to him. When I get up there he's sitting in his underpants at his computer, playing Phantom Flyer. "I'm at thirty thousand feet, and I just lost an engine," he says. "Not only that, my flaps are stuck. I'm going into a dive." On the computer screen the horizon line bobs up and down in the windshield of a jet cockpit. Finally it flies right up out of sight and the earth gets closer and closer. "This always happens," he sighs, leaning back and scratching his ribs until his plane hits the ground. We watch the colorful explosion together. "How about we go catch some breakfast?" he says.

"Dwight, are you crazy? I'm trying to help Anita fix this tape. I'm starting to think you have a self-destructive streak, Dwight."

He stands up and wanders over to the sofa bed. "I'm starting to think you're a worrywart," he replies, and begins to dress from the pile of garments on the floor. Dwight's taste in clothing is the stuff of legend. Today he's wearing the fruits of a recent sweep through Filene's Basement: pearl-gray over-the-calf hose, decorated with flying yellow geese, and maroon Italian loafers. He puts on the shoes before he puts on the pants—the shoes being delicate enough, and the electric-blue rayon trousers baggy enough, to allow for that—and finishes with a pink T-shirt that says OFFICIAL JAMAICAN BIKINI INSPECTOR. Then he puts his arm around my shoulders. "Fixing this tape is beside the point," he says.

"Oh, really," I say.

"Yes. Would you like me to tell you why?"

"Sure. Tell me."

"First you show me those home fries and eggs. And that ham."

Dwight's favorite diner is called the Pig 'n' Poke, over by the railway switching yards beneath the Mass Pike. From our booth, I can see a blue Conrail locomotive pulling boxcars through a tunnel.

Dwight piles fried egg onto a corner of toast and raises it in the air. "The tape you made with Anita was perfectly competent," he says, and he pushes the toast-egg assembly into his mouth.

I should be having something wholesome myself, not the French fries and root beer I've ordered. But taking real nourishment seems out of keeping with my present circumstances.

"The Doctor and I admired it when we watched it last night," Dwight goes on. "You could find work all over town with a demo reel of stuff like that. You could stop working for us and go make the same boring video everybody else is making. Yak about something, then show a picture of it. Yak some more, show another picture. Yak, picture, yak, picture, yak, picture, yak."

"That's what clients think a video is, Dwight. That's what they want."

He slices a piece of ham and folds it in half. "The first thing to remember about clients," he says, "is that they don't know what they want. The second thing—this is the problem part—is that they think they do." He pops the ham in.

"What about the third thing?" I say.

"What third thing?"

"That a lot of money is getting spent, and it's their money."

"Wrong!" Dwight exclaims, pounding the table with the butt of his knife. The sugar shaker falls down and trickles a white mound next to the napkins like time running out. "Wrong, wrong, wrong. They signed a contract. That money belongs to us."

"Well, then the videotape is theirs."

"Nope, that's ours too. We're its creators." He picks up the fallen shaker and streams sugar into his cup. Then he stirs it and has a sip. "Wow, that's sweet," he says. "The third thing about clients—the real third thing—is that if you let them, they'll start doing your job for you. But they don't know how to do your job, see? And so in the end they're disappointed and it's your fault."

"They probably wouldn't have been disappointed, Dwight. They probably would have liked it, and we'd practically be done by now."

"That's even worse. Then we'd have to feel bad all alone, knowing we took the cheesy way out. A household of hacks with only themselves for comfort." He motions to the waitress for our check. "No," he says, "what we have to do is correctly identify our job and then do it. Now, what is our job?"

"To make a videotape."

He shakes his head. "Anybody could do that." He gets up with the check to pay it. "Our job is to be the brilliant media wizards."

Outside, I stop at the passenger door of Dwight's white '64 Bonneville—it's the only car he can find that's big enough for him to drive—but he strides right past it and out to the highway. "Where are you going?" I say, but he refuses to answer me. I have to run through traffic to catch him on the median strip.

"We have some research to do," he says.

Across the highway is a shopping center with an amusement arcade. I follow Dwight into a dim, cavernous space full of flashing machines and teenagers in T-shirts decorated with skulls and lightning bolts. The proprietor is behind the cash register in a dirty barber's smock. He waves greetings to Dwight, slaps a roll of quarters into one of Dwight's outstretched hands, plucks a ten-dollar bill from the other. Then Dwight leads me to a video game called Jungle Bungle. He taps the screen with his fingernail. On it is a list of the highest scores. Dwight's initials are two numbers from the top, next to yesterday's date.

"Yesterday? I thought you were out on a shoot yesterday."

"I was," he says. "But I must have had some free time." He puts two quarters in the machine. "OK, I'd like to hear a little meditation on computer software."

"I can't work this way, Dwight."

"We're falling on our faces with a big client today, bud, and you're the writer on this project."

He begins to play the game. The star of Jungle Bungle is an animated ape whose great joy in life is bananas. The player moves a joystick to make the ape run around and collect bananas and put them in a sack. At first it's easy— the yellow fruit is simply lying on the ground or hanging in bunches low in the trees. A few flicks of the joystick and

Dwight has every banana there is. Then the machine plays
a little tune and a new landscape slides into view.

"Insights?" Dwight asks. "Inspirations?"

"Dwight, this is totally irrelevant."

"How can you say that?" he says. "What about our client's sacred product? Isn't it the same thing? You travel
around in a kind of environment and play with information
—take a piece from here and move it over there. You know
where they got that idea?"

"No."

Dwight's ape is now hunkering on the banks of a wide,
fast-moving river.

"From ancient computer games," he says, "the ones the
programmers played on the mainframes when they were
college kids. You think it's gonna stop there? Five years
from now, business software will look just like Jungle Bungle. Trust me. The future always arrives as a game."

A riverboat appears with a magnificent freight of bananas. The ape clambers down to the water's edge to swim
to the boat, but the black, humpy backs of many crocodiles
surface in the river, and he scurries back up the bank. Then
Dwight makes his move. He runs to the water and leaps
right onto the nearest crocodile. When it turns around to
bite him, Dwight bounds to the next and then the next,
and in this way he makes it all the way to the boat, grabs
the bananas, and, vaulting from monster to monster, comes
all the way back. "First time I tried that I got eaten," he
says happily.

Jungle environments come and go, with Dwight inge-
niously racking up banana points. It's not until the eighth
or ninth landscape that he finally makes a mistake, opening

the wrong door in a temple full of fruit. Then it's my turn. Immediately, little monkeys in the trees drop coconuts on me and knock me out. Dwight's turn again, and he zips through the landscapes even faster than before. "The ape has to learn certain things," he says, "or he doesn't get to the next level of the game. But, of course, saying 'The ape has to learn' is like saying the computer 'knows' this or that."

"It's you who have to learn certain things."

"You bet. But in seeing it as the ape's situation you get this peculiar distance on yourself."

"It becomes something apart from you," I say.

"*You* become something apart from you."

"You become the ape."

"Yes!" Dwight says.

We return from the amusement arcade to find a metallic-khaki BMW sitting in the drive. Dwight runs the Bonneville up onto the curb, jumps out, and dashes onto the porch and into the house. Even from outside I can hear him slamming upstairs in his usual way, three steps at a time.

"And here's Walter!" Anita says when I step into the editing suite. "Walter's our writer. He wrote this script."

"Oh," the clients say, "the writer," and they shake my hand—two men and a woman about my age. They're all wearing gray business suits, but it's easy to pick out the alpha male. He shakes my hand much harder than the beta male does, talks like a drill sergeant, and shoots laser eye-beams into my face. The beta male has an open, friendly nature—a classic beta trait.

The Doctor has been teaching me the theory of creatures in groups. He's a scholar of such things, and it seems to serve him well. He winks at me from across the room. The Doctor himself is an alpha male, but a special breed whose alpha strategy is to pretend that he isn't.

Anita has polished up the golden Emmy statues and arranged them on a shelf above the editing table. I nudge her over there with my hip. "I didn't write one word of this and you know it," I whisper. She gives my ribs a little squeeze. "It's showtime!" she announces, handing out yellow legal pads.

We settle into the expensive office chairs, and she lets the video roll. A helicopter shoots the company's headquarters at dawn, we go inside for a vérité-like tour, programmers have lunch in the cafeteria and say mysterious things, the employee volleyball team plays a game to some tasty electric jazz. I hear furious scratching on the legal pads. Five minutes in, the alpha male wants Anita to stop the tape.

"No stopping," she says. "It breaks up the flow."

I should be thinking about damage control, but instead I'm thinking that Anita's talents are as wasted on corporate PR as they were on documentaries. She's more like the queen of video rock and roll. Her ending is a great scene of software people at their terminals arguing about the best place to get Chinese food. Then the screen goes blank.

"Are you people out of your minds?" the alpha male says. "This isn't what we talked about. This isn't what you said you were going to do. What about the story we agreed on?"

"There's tons of story in there," Anita says. "Don't you think?"

"What happened to all the shots of the president at his desk?"

This often happens at these screenings—the first problem is that their boss isn't in it enough. "They were dull," I say, sniffing for emphasis. You have to be looking for it, but even with the air-conditioner on and the windows closed, the slightest trace of skunk is still discernible. "What did you want, the same boring video everybody else is making?"

"But he's not in it at all!" the woman says. "He happens to be the founder of this company."

"When I was working in the bush," the Doctor says, "I often observed the wisest rulers not taking part in certain rituals. They enjoyed the spectacle of the ceremonial tribe."

"Other reactions?" Dwight says.

The beta male pipes up. "I thought it had some great energy," he says. "It made the company seem like fun."

The alpha male shoots him an unmistakable look of shut-your-face. "The product isn't even mentioned once!" he exclaims. "This was supposed to be about the bugs. You were supposed to talk about how this new version of the product eliminates all those bugs."

"People don't want to hear about bugs," Dwight says.

"That's right," I put in. "Haven't they heard enough?"

The alpha male gets out of his chair. "We tell you what

we want and we leave you alone, and you get freaky on us. I'm giving you a week to fix this tape."

"Fixing this tape is beside the point," I say.

"Oh, really," he says.

"Anybody can puff a product," Dwight says. "We're vision people. We work with the big themes."

"Fine," the alpha male says. "You have a week to find one."

He snaps his briefcase shut and stomps off to the stairs with his colleagues in line behind him. Only the friendly beta male turns to wave goodbye. We peek down to the street through the venetian blinds and watch them drive away.

The Doctor puts his arm around Anita's shoulders. "Rough cuts are always—you know—rough," he says.

"Rough?" Anita says. "I think we just entered lawsuit territory."

"The other guy liked it," I say, but Anita just shakes her head. I've never seen her so discouraged.

"Is anybody hungry?" Dwight inquires.

"I could eat a little something," the Doctor says.

Chinese food always cheers Anita up. "Kung-pao chicken?" I say to her. "Scallops in spicy garlic sauce? Szechuan shrimp?"

"I don't want anything," she says.

"All the more Hunan octopus for me," Dwight says, leading us down the stairs.

It proves to be a pretty summer afternoon, with the heat letting up and blue sky and puffs of cloud above the mostly brown two- and three-family houses that line our street. I tap Dwight's shoulder. "Can we talk about something? Tenant to landlord?"

"Uh-oh," he says, following me down the drive.

I take him around back where we keep the garbage barrels. They're on their sides, lids off, bags ripped open. Trash is strewn across the ground like the past rushing before our eyes—every piece of junk mail we've received this week mingled with the remains of all the food we've eaten. And hovering above the devastation is the abiding aura of skunk.

"I bought these really good garbage cans," Dwight says.

"I think the raccoons help them take off the lids," I say. "They have thumbs or something."

"I just want to point out that if we start killing them we're going up against the whole ecosystem. There must be thousands on the waiting list for the next available house."

"I don't want to kill them," I say.

"Good," Dwight says, heading back up the drive. "Let's clean it up later." And then, gazing out over the rooftops, he says, "Why do they have to mess with our minds?"

"The skunks?"

"No, these people," he sighs, flapping his hand at the sky.

It's still Happy Hour when we arrive at the Chinese place our videotaped programmers voted the best. A lovely young woman brings our drinks. Perhaps on account of her loveliness we order too much food, and only items printed in red.

"To Anita, our brilliant producer!" I say, raising my glass.

"To Anita!" Dwight and the Doctor chime in.

Anita drinks up and gives us a smile. She's coming out of it. "I wish Rebecca could have made it to dinner," she says to the table at large. And then, to me, she adds, "Rebecca loves hot food."

"Anita, I'm just wondering," I say. "Is there any reason to think that Rebecca might have made it to dinner? Tonight, I mean?"

"Oh, well, she was supposed to stop by this afternoon, that's all. But with Rebecca you never know."

"He knows that," Dwight says.

"I've told her all about you," Anita says.

"Just nod your head," Dwight says.

"Rebecca's very nice," the Doctor says. "Who have you got lined up for me?"

"I thought you were promised to a chieftain's daughter," Anita says.

"I am. But you can have many wives in that culture."

The food arrives and we lay into it, chopsticks and beer bottles flashing in the air. Our eyes water and our noses liquify, and we never let our glasses get empty.

"I'm a simple person," the Doctor says, once we've begun to slow down. He always says that when he's about to take charge. "I was in the bank the other day and they couldn't tell me how much money I had. You know why?"

"Let me guess," Dwight says. "We're getting too dependent on technology."

"Cars are OK," the Doctor says. "I like my toaster oven. But there's something creepy about computer stuff. I can't relate to it."

"Well, it's totally nonhuman," I say.

"Don't say that," Anita says. "We can't say nonhuman."

"But isn't it true?" I say. "If you think about it, the blind faith is almost unbelievable. People trust their whole lives—*their money*—to these incomprehensible creations beyond their control. When have human beings ever trusted anything like that?"

Dwight rises from his chair with a peculiar smile, squinting as though dazzled by brilliant lights. "I just had an idea," he says. "I have to go call somebody."

The fortune cookies come while he's on the phone. Anita and the Doctor receive identical predictions: great success awaits them around the corner. Dwight returns to find that he will meet an influential stranger. "Your friends are your greatest wealth," I read aloud from my own slip of paper, and we drain our glasses in a toast to that. Then I put the fortune in my wallet for safekeeping. It actually says, You Will Have a Long and Happy File.

Outside, a thin orange line remains in the sky to the west. In the Bonneville, the stick-on digital dashboard clock says 2:17 without specifying morning or afternoon. It's wrong either way; we're driving home in a twilight the pearl gray of Dwight's new socks.

"Can I fix this tape in one week?" Anita asks.

"I was thinking you could, and then you said that," the Doctor says, sitting next to me in the back.

Dwight is taking a strange way home. In a neighborhood unknown to me he parks in front of a broken-down triple-decker. "I have to borrow a piece of equipment," he says, running into the house, and then he emerges with a big cardboard box, which he stows in the trunk. When we pull into our drive, he says, "I'd like to have a little partners' meeting upstairs right now. Walter, while we're doing that would you mind cleaning up the garbage out back?"

"Sure, Dwight," I say. "You guys have a meeting, I clean up the trash."

He gives me his famous smile and pinches my cheek. "You're playing a very important role," he says.

In the backyard I make sure I'm working alone—skunks have no fear and maybe no brains, and if you're not careful you can saunter right onto their heads—and then I scrape up the garbage with a shovel and broom. The little enforcers have been systematic, no coffee filter left unturned. I'm hosing down the blacktop and rinsing off my hands when the Doctor appears, humping two big cases of lighting gear down the driveway.

"Guess what?" he says, heading into the backyard. "We're having a little shoot."

"Now?" I say.

"Exciting, isn't it?" Anita says brightly, coming after him with her computer screen in her hands. Dwight brings up the rear with a folding table and the big orange extension cord. He sets those things down and crooks a finger to beckon me back up the driveway.

"Now, Dwight? We're having a shoot now?"

"Inspiration doesn't punch a clock, Walter. You know that. Plus, this idea has to be shot at night. It won't have the same spooky look in the daytime."

"Oh. Am I working on the script out here?"

"No, you're not." He opens his trunk, takes out the big box, and walks to the house. "Let's go to your place," he says on the porch. I open the door and follow him down the hall to my room. He drops the box on my bed. "How do you feel, Walter?" he asks.

"I feel great," I say.

"Good. Close your eyes," he says. "It's a surprise."

I close my eyes. Dwight holds something fuzzy up under my chin. I open my eyes again. A great expanse of black fur spreads from my neck to the floor. I peek into the opened cardboard box. It contains the head of a gorilla.

"What's this for, Dwight? Who's gonna wear this?"

He looks at me the way you look at a child; then he lays the furry body in my arms and rests the head on top. "Congratulations, Walter. You'll be directed by the lovely Anita."

I've had bad parts before, but always within my own species. I don't even know how you do this. "Do I keep my shoes on?" I ask.

"You don't keep anything on," Dwight says. "This is an action role in a heavy outfit. You'll be too hot if you're dressed in there. Plus, you'll feel more feral without your pants." He holds up an outstretched hand. "You're on in five," he says, and waves goodbye.

I get out of my clothes and into the suit. Powerful polyester fumes envelop me; I smell like new wall-to-wall carpet. I stand before the full-length closet mirror. Sticking out of the enormous black body, my little human face looks pathetic, so I put on the head, and when I consult the mirror again a change takes place in the chemistry of my brain. I bound out of the bedroom, huge shoulders squeezing through the doorway. The kitchen is flooded with white light, the window as bright as a television screen. My friends are in the backyard, arranging Anita's computer on the table at the edge of the lawn. I pad out to the enclosed back porch and watch them for a minute from there. Then I leap down into the lights and roar.

"Walter!" Anita cries. "I can't believe it! I can't believe how incredible you look! It is you, isn't it, Walter? *Walter?*"

I swipe at the air and run across the grass. The Doctor hoists the camera to his shoulder. "Kalimba, lord of the jungle!" he proclaims. "No creature dare trifle with mighty Kalimba!"

They have a small color monitor propped on the equipment cases so Anita can watch the framing of the shots. I lumber over there to see myself in it. I scratch my ribs and beat my chest. *"Hey,"* I say. *"I do look pretty scary, don't I?"* But inside the big, hollow head my voice is muffled and indistinct.

"Ruh, ruh, ruh," Dwight says, imitating the way I sound.

I hear an unfamiliar voice and spin around. A strange woman is standing in the shadows beside me. I jump back in surprise, lose my footing in the cumbersome suit, and fall down on the ground. Anita rushes over to help me up. "Kalimba," she says, managing to stop laughing for a moment, "this is Rebecca. Rebecca, Kalimba. Kalimba's the guy I've been telling you about," she says, and then she cracks up again.

Rebecca is wearing black jeans and a light-blue silky top and smiling very weakly. I put out my paw to shake her hand. She steps away and waves instead and puts her hands behind her back.

"My name is actually Walter," I say, waving in return. *"Can you hang around for a while? Until we finish this shoot? Maybe we could have a drink or something."*

"What's he saying?" Rebecca asks Anita.

"Beats me," Anita says. "We can't understand you, ape boy."

"Maybe if you took off your head," Rebecca suggests.

"Time to get to work, Kalimba," Dwight calls out. "No socializing with the females."

"Hide behind those bushes," Anita says. "I'll give you a cue."

A wall of scrappy hedges lines the property's rear edge, long stalks of jungly sumac trees sprouting up in the gaps. I crawl through and hide in the neighbor's backyard. Dwight trains the lights on my hiding place. The Doctor gets into position with the camera. And then Anita cries, "Kalimba, claw your way out through the trees!"

I burst through the vegetation and do my best King Kong in the lights, flailing and howling. Then I act amazed to see Anita's PC. I stalk it on all fours.

She improvises in a narrator's voice. *"Do you sometimes think computers weren't made for human beings?"* she says. *"Are you tired of searching for the right business software? Well, take a look at our products.* OK, Kalimba, look at the computer screen. Scratch your head. *They're certainly not primitive.* Now play with the computer. Tap on the keyboard and stuff. Great. Now jump up and down and act real happy. *But they're so easy to use, even a monkey can do it."*

I nod my head up and down and dance all around in apelike wonder. I point to the computer screen. I pound the ground with my feet. *"It's not an easy life for me here, Rebecca,"* I say. *"I slave over video scripts night and day, and then as soon as I finish one they change their minds and make me do it again. If things don't turn out right, I have to do this."*

"Ruh, ruh, ruh, ruh," Dwight says.

"We're rolling, Kalimba," Anita says. "Do more ape things."

I play with the computer again, acting out big monkey excitement over the shapes and colors on the screen. I lope across the lawn on my knuckles. I cling to the Empire State Building and swipe at the airplanes around my head. And then, while plucking nits out of my coat, I notice two big skunks sniffing around by the garbage cans. Dwight catches me looking and he looks too, and then he swings a movie light onto the racing-striped creatures. They sit up and blink their vacant little eyes.

"Get them!" Anita calls to the Doctor, and he moves in for the shot. *"We won't comment on our competition,"* she narrates. *"But we've seen them lurking around."*

"Hey, those are skunks!" Rebecca cries.

"Isn't it great?" Anita says. "They live here. They're ours."

But Rebecca panics and tries to run away across the grass. Dwight, always the heads-up producer, spins the Doctor around by his shirt so he can shoot her doing that. And me, I don't even need direction for this. Life is a video for me now. I step into Rebecca's path and sweep her up in my arms.

"Let us save you from our competitors!" Anita shouts.

Rebecca screams and kicks and demands that I let her go. But Dwight throws a handful of popcorn at my feet, the oblivious skunks mosey right over to get it, and Rebecca yields to my furry embrace. I glance down to watch the skunks having their snack. Seeing them up close like this is doing something odd to my mind. It's bringing back my dream—reminding me that skunks were my only companions when Jeanette turned me away from her door.

"Rebecca, you're doing great," I say. *"I think you have real star potential. Don't tell me you've never acted before."*

I look out across the yard at Anita and Dwight and the Doctor. I've never seen them so happy. I say to myself: Kalimba, these are the people who helped you when you were a miserable, lonely wreck. They gave you a new shot at life. They taught you their glamorous profession. These are your friends, Kalimba, your greatest wealth. And now what do they ask from you in return? Only that you stand in the bright movie lights with a woman in your arms and be everybody's charming hero.

"Relationships take faith and hope and cooperation," Anita narrates. *"We're a big software company, but we think of ourselves as a gentle giant. You can trust us with your precious data."*

Isn't it true?

CITIZENS

Halfway up the hill, Jesse sat down in the mud
and started to cry. Mark picked him up and pointed him
toward the top, where the green crest of the hill met the
open blue sky. Jesse had been willing to climb there before,
but now he wasn't. He kept letting his legs buckle beneath
him, making Mark hold him up by his underarms. They
were standing on the slope this way when Mark felt a
tremor run through the ground and the air. Before he could
realize what it was, one of the army helicopters bounced up
into the sky from behind the other side of the hill. The
sudden huge appearance of it frightened him—he could
feel his heart chopping just like the aircraft. He expected
Jesse to get hysterical as the thing roared over their heads,
but the spectacle of the helicopter and the pulsing concus-
sion of its sound seemed to erase everything in Jesse's

mind; he gaped blankly at the flying machine, tracking it with his eyes as it whizzed away. Mark was sure the men up there were taking his picture with telephoto lenses. He considered showing them his middle finger; then he thought better of it. He put Jesse over his shoulder and struggled up the wet, grassy slope. Jesse was five years old now, and he wasn't light.

At the top, Mark spread out their blanket and sat Jesse down. Then he strolled along the ridge, looking out over the land that couldn't be seen from the park below—the colorful geometry of farms and vineyards to the west and, to the east, the vast, uniform tract of the army depot. It was beautiful country, and on that account he was sorry to be leaving it. But then again these fine vistas weren't part of life down where he lived, somewhere out there to the north. Jesse started to cry again; his diaper needed changing. Mark slipped out of his backpack and rummaged in it for one of the extra Pampers. Then he had the amusing thought of a surveillance photograph of his son's dirty diaper, and he decided to wait for one of the choppers to come around again.

He sat on the blanket next to Jesse and looked into the grassy valley where they'd been, a natural amphitheater defined by a range of hills and a lake. An enormous mass of people covered the floor of the valley in front of a large stage at the foot of the opposite hill. Earlier, Mark had listened to the news on Linda's headphone radio; the army estimated the crowd to be ten thousand. From up here it was plain that twice that many were actually there. Mark could hear the thin, distant sound of the rock band that was performing onstage at the moment.

Linda was still down there somewhere. She'd wanted to wander around in the crowd awhile before meeting up for lunch. Mark got his binoculars from the backpack and looked along the lines of media vehicles and propaganda tables near the access roads to the park. People were selling food and drink at some of the tables, and T-shirts printed with stop-the-missiles slogans and designs. The Hare Krishnas were on hand, wending their way single file through the protesters, chanting and praying. They were easy to spot in their saffron robes. Mark was too far away to make out faces, but he soon recognized Linda—not so much by her white pants and pink sweatshirt, he realized, as by the way she carried herself. Something about Linda's presence made her leap out of a crowd for him, even at this distance. But that had more to do with familiarity, Mark thought, than with some unusual attraction; it didn't necessarily prove that they were meant for each other. Linda was talking to a bearded man behind a socialist literature table, gesturing with her hands the way she did when she was trying to express her most heartfelt idea about something. Her American flag was fluttering on its stick from the back pocket of her painter's pants.

Mark had one of the flags too, planted in the ground next to the blanket; more than half the people down there had them. They'd been given out free at the entrance to the park, each one with a slip of paper stapled to the wooden dowel that read, LET'S TAKE BACK THE FLAG! Tonight's television coverage of the rally would show an ocean of nuclear protesters waving American flags. When Mark first took part in events like this—the antiwar demonstrations that were going full blast when he finished his hitch in the army—the organizers weren't so sophisticated. Something about the new sophistication saddened Mark, but he understood the strength and smartness of it, the necessity to think strategically if you wanted to survive.

He was glad he'd brought Jesse along. When the maniacs destroyed the world, it would have the same effect on Jesse as on everyone else. Jesse would never know that, but that was another good reason for his being here—in his frailty and obliviousness Jesse was just like most citizens of his country, as much like them as he'd ever be. Mark knew that some people would see a boy like Jesse on the TV news tonight and think of him only as further proof that something was wrong with the protesters. But other people might see him and understand.

Mark put down the binoculars. Jesse had crawled off the blanket and was eating a handful of mud and grass. He looked up and laughed when he heard his father call his name. Then he threw the mud and grass onto the blanket and clapped his hands. Mark shook the blanket clean and put Jesse back on it. He wiped out Jesse's mouth with a paper towel. Then he noticed two army helicopters vectoring his way from different directions, and he smiled and began to unbutton Jesse's pants.

Linda sat down on the blanket and stuck her American flag in the ground next to Mark's. She called Jesse's name and shook one of his feet. He liked that and waved his arms at her. Mark was sitting with his back to Linda, one of his legs thrown over Jesse's middle to keep him from running away. He was using the binoculars to look at the army depot across the highway where the latest missiles were supposed to be stored, the ones that could practically turn a corner on a city street or fly into a living room window.

"I'm back," Linda said.

"I saw you coming," Mark said.

"Can you see anything over there?" Linda asked. "Can you see any of the rockets?"

Mark looked at her over his shoulder. Then he went back to the binoculars. "You must be kidding," he said. "Do you really think they just leave them lying around in plain view like Tinkertoys or something?"

"I thought maybe with the binoculars you could see them," Linda said. "Some people down there are saying that they're not really keeping them here, that the army just wants us to think they're here."

"They're here," Mark said.

"Well, if you can't see them, what are you looking at?"

"I'm looking at a guard in a watchtower. I think he's looking at me. Be a good soldier, boy. Pace back and forth real nice like they taught you."

"I got you a Nuclear Freeze button," Linda said.

"Great," Mark said.

"I brought back some pamphlets, too. There's one put out by the vets. It has some stuff in it about Agent Orange."

"Terrific," Mark said.

Linda said, "After you left I thought I saw Sarah and Phil. But it turned out to be somebody else."

Mark dropped the binoculars and let them swing from the strap around his neck. Then he twisted himself around until he was facing Linda. Sarah was Jesse's mother.

"Linda," he said, "why do you have to invent things just to have something to say? You know they're not here. You know they wouldn't come to something like this."

"I'm not inventing anything," Linda said. "For a minute I thought I saw them, that's all. When I thought it was them, I thought how funny it would be if they were here."

"It wouldn't be funny," Mark said.

"OK, Mark," Linda said.

Jesse lived with Sarah and her second husband, Phil. For a long time after his divorce, Mark didn't even see his son. Then, when he and Linda moved in together about a year ago, they started keeping Jesse every other weekend. This wasn't one of their regular weekends, but Mark wanted to spend an extra day with him. When he called Sarah to arrange it, she'd made passing mention of the big antimissiles demonstration and then waited to see what Mark would say. Since she wasn't honest enough to come right out and ask if he planned to go, Mark pretended not to be interested in the rally. Sarah would have objected to his bringing Jesse to such a thing.

In two weeks, Sarah was putting Jesse into a home. A week after that, Mark was moving away. He'd sworn never to let his son go into one of those places, and he tried to take custody when Sarah said she couldn't care for Jesse at home anymore. At the custody hearing, the woman from the state agency flustered Mark with harsh questions and statements about Jesse and himself. The woman had had plenty of poison poured in her ears, and she made Mark's declarations of love and duty seem petty and dishonest. The woman said that Mark was still trying to blame Sarah for the way Jesse was, that he was trying to punish her by fighting for the baby, that he really wasn't the kind of man prepared to sacrifice his life to a boy like Jesse. Mark turned to his ex-wife and denied these things to her face, but Sarah only looked away. Then the woman from the state went down her list of hard facts—that Mark wasn't married to the girl he was living with, that there was no evidence of regular advancement in his job, that he frequented bars, that last year he'd been stopped for drunk driving.

When the hearing was over, Mark felt as though he'd had his insides stolen out of him. Driving home, he saw the whole town as a sad cartoon, a place people only imagined themselves to be living. He hadn't really been alive here all these years. He pulled up in front of his apartment building, and it looked like something from a movie set.

He had a friend from army electronics school who worked for Motorola in Phoenix. Ever since the service, the friend had been raving to Mark about the Sun Belt, about the wonderfully different life people lived down there. The friend had always said that Mark could walk right into something good at Motorola. By the time Mark climbed the stairs to his apartment that day, he'd moved to Arizona in his mind.

Linda was going to Phoenix with him. They'd both simply assumed she would go, and it had been a great relief to have something not be a struggle. Their simple assumption had felt like cool water percolating up through jagged rocks, clear evidence of hope and goodness. But now— sitting on top of a hill where he could see for miles in any direction, twenty thousand people below him trying to change history and his son next to him on a blanket not knowing who he was—Mark saw that assumptions were only evidence of weakness and fear. He felt encrusted with them. He wasn't sure anymore that Linda should go to Phoenix with him, that he had any business walking into the future with this particular woman. He could almost feel all the assumptions he'd ever made clinging inside him like deposits inside arteries and veins. They were the bad residue of the past, the thing that killed you. He wanted to scrape all the assumptions out of his life.

He turned to Linda and began to speak to her about it. He tried to express himself precisely, but he ended up blurting it all out in a few sentences that sounded bad. When he finished, Linda just sat there on the blanket for a minute without saying anything. Then she unpacked their lunch from Mark's backpack and gave Jesse a peanut butter and jelly sandwich. He chortled and ripped the sandwich to pieces, and then he squished one of the pieces between his hands like clay.

"As if I didn't have plenty of doubts myself," Linda said at last.

"I didn't know that," Mark said.

"Well, now you know," she said. "It all scares me just as much as it scares you. It just doesn't scare me as much as that." She pointed in the direction of the army depot. "Perspective," she said bitterly, and then she began to cry.

"Perspective," Mark said, nodding his head.

Linda pulled the lid off a yogurt container. "If you want to back out," she said, "you can back out."

"Some kind of weird mood has settled on me," Mark said. "I can't think until I shake it off."

"Oh, well, you just take your time," Linda said. "But do

you think you'll be able to shake it off before we load the U-Haul and drive away? Do you think you could make up your mind before then? Just as a courtesy?"

"That's not fair," Mark said. "You're not trying to understand."

"I'm not?" Linda said. "I've given my notice at work, I've packed all my books and half my clothes. Five minutes ago I was moving to Phoenix. I've never even been to Phoenix before." She dropped the open yogurt container on the blanket and put her face in her hands. "Jesus Christ," she said.

"I'm sorry," Mark said. "I need to get out from under this mood."

"You just let me know when you do, Mark," Linda said.

Mark scooted across the blanket and put his arm around Linda's shoulders. He kissed her and then he put the side of his head next to hers, the way people do in wedding portraits or Calypso dance routines. He turned the binoculars around backward and put one big lens to Linda's eye, one to his. At the end of a long, dark tunnel, Mark could see his tiny son. Jesse had Linda's yogurt in his hands. He was scooping the plain white yogurt out of the container and dropping it onto the blanket. When all the yogurt was out, he began to eat the blueberry preserves from the bottom.

"See that?" Mark said. "See what he's doing? He knows they put the good stuff underneath all the other stuff."

"He's always known that," Linda said. "That's not new. Blueberry's his favorite. Hey, blueberry boy," she called out to Jesse as if across a mountain pass, but Jesse didn't pay any attention.

Down in the park, the music had stopped, and now a man was at the microphone speaking out against nuclear war. Mark and Linda could hear something like the ghosts of his words, but most of what he actually said was lost in the big open sky. They took their heads away from the binoculars and listened to the man anyway.

"Rhetoric," Mark said after some time. "All completely true, all necessary to say again and again. But why doesn't somebody tell me something I don't already know?"

Linda got up and cleaned the yogurt off the blanket.

"I'm tired," she said. "I feel sick, too. I'm going to take a nap."

"We never had lunch," Mark said. "You'll feel better if you have lunch."

"I'm not hungry. You go ahead and eat. Wake me up when the bands start playing again."

"Maybe we should just go home," Mark said. "I feel like going home."

"Not me," Linda said. "I like it here. I want to listen to the music and dance for peace with my fellow citizens. That's what I came here to do. That's how Jesse and me are going to save the world. Right, Jesse?"

Jesse was lying on his side on the blanket with one of his arms thrown over his head.

"I'm taking him home," Mark said.

"He's happy here," Linda said. "He wants to stay right here with me."

"That's ridiculous, Linda. He doesn't know where he is. He doesn't even know who you are."

"He knows more than you think," Linda said. "You treat him like he doesn't know anything, but he knows plenty of things. He knows what we're talking about right now. You've been treating him wrong."

"Don't you ever say that," Mark said. "That's a lie."

"It's true," Linda said. "Isn't it, Jesse?" She stretched out on the blanket next to the child and took him in her arms. "Let's snuggle up for a nap, baby boy," she said, "and then we can go dancing later."

Mark got up onto his hands and knees. "You'd actually turn my own son against me," he said. "Well, I'm not letting you do that. Jesse, listen to me. This is your father speaking. Maybe I've been wrong. Maybe I should have tried to talk to you before. I didn't want things to be this way. There's another whole side to this story. I want you to listen to me now."

He pulled Jesse from Linda's arms and rolled him on his back to get his full attention. But Jesse had already fallen sound asleep on his own—blueberry preserves smeared all over his face, his hand stuck inside the yogurt container as though muffling the clapper of a bell.

MONARCHS

Early this morning, in a dream he was having, a woman appeared in Guy's kitchen asking for something to eat. Guy didn't think he knew this woman, and he couldn't really see her face, but he understood that she was immensely beautiful, wise, and kind. The woman wasn't asking to eat simply anything. She wanted a completely new food, something she'd never eaten before. In the dream it was breakfast time. Guy opened his refrigerator, inspiration flapped out, and the meal he prepared came through vividly in the dream, with all its colors and aromas —poached eggs on toasted zucchini bread with a fresh cilantro salsa and sliced white grapes. Just as he was about to eat his own portion, Guy awoke in a rapture, seeing and smelling everything except the woman. He came downstairs to the guest room June and I are using, woke me up, and described the dream food to me—the pungent herbs mingling with the sweetness of the bread, the tart, crisp contrast of the grapes, the egg yolk rushing out to meet the dawn. Half asleep, I said it didn't sound all that bad.

I'm at the corner market now, buying the grapes. Guy wants to surprise Vita and June with the dream breakfast. We found all the ingredients in his fridge, just the way they were in his sleep—except that the real-life grapes had slipped their earthly bonds in the crisper drawer.

A little old Italian lady named Mom runs the corner store. That's what the whole neighborhood calls her—Mom. There used to be a Pop, but he's gone; Mom takes care of the store alone now. She finishes ringing up a customer and comes over to help me. June and I were in here with Guy the other day; she recognizes me as his friend.

"Morning, Mom," I say.

"Hello, bad one," she says. She's about four feet tall and has to look almost straight up to scowl at me. "I see you," she says. "You just-a wake up now. Where's-a you house? When-a you go to church?"

"I don't live around here, Mom," I say. "I'm on vacation. I'm visiting your *paisano.*" I tilt my head toward Guy's house up the street and make the motions of clicking a camera. Guy's people and Mom's people come from nearby towns in the south of Italy. They're always gabbing about the old country. When he went to Europe a couple of years ago, Guy visited Mom's hometown, took pictures of everything, and made huge prints for her when he got back. In Mom's book, Guy is tops.

"Where's-a that one?" she says, clicking the make-believe camera.

"He's cooking breakfast for us," I say. Mom nods her approval of this. "He sent me to see you about some grapes. The seedless ones." I point to the fruit section where she has a few bunches of white grapes. They don't look so good, too many brown and wrinkled ones on each bunch.

She picks up one of the bunches and shakes her head. Then she drops it back in the bin. "I get for you," she says, and shuffles off to the back of the store.

Mom is a photo opportunity herself, and this has not been lost on Guy. He's taken her picture many times, lurking in the aisles with his Leica while she stocks the shelves or works the register. When he had his museum show in New York last year, Guy used some of his portraits of Mom and the museum made one of them into a postcard—Mom in her cat-lady eyeglasses and a frumpy print dress like the one she must have worn on Ellis Island, smiling with the last of her teeth and holding up a big head of Bibb lettuce. I'm not sure if Mom knows about that—that strangers exchange her picture in the mail.

She comes out of the back room with her arms full of grapes, looking like an aged version of the Sun-Maid raisin girl. I help her arrange them in their bin; then she selects the nicest bunch for me.

"You wife make for you?" she says, touching her head and then running her hand down to her hip. She means June's long straight hair.

"No, Mom," I say. "Guy is making breakfast. Guy. Your friend."

"Where's-a you wife?" Mom asks.

"She's sleeping."

Mom looks at the clock on the wall and shakes her head.

Then she looks at my hands, where no ring is to be seen. "How long-a you marry?"

The numerical part of that question is easy. I counted it just yesterday. "Five years," I say.

"How many children, you?" Mom asks.

"No children, Mom."

Now she really gets aggravated with me. She slaps herself on the forehead. "You no wear-a you ring. You no have-a children. What's-a matter for you?"

I shrug my shoulders and smile and hand her some money for the grapes. "I don't know, Mom."

She gives me my change. "You do right," she says, shaking her finger at me, but I can tell she thinks of me as lost.

"I will, Mom," I say. "Don't worry."

Outside, in front of the store with my little sackful of grapes, I stop to take a long, deep breath. Summer's over; it's really fall now. Already the sugar maples have lost some of their red leaves. Before long, Guy will be out shooting this neighborhood transformed by enormous overlays of snow. But this morning is one of those dry, brilliant ones they get upstate in this season. The sunshine seems hollow and buoyant as the bones of birds, and somehow it conveys that ethereal loft to everything it touches. The neat, modest houses on their uniform plots, the parked cars, the big evergreens, the sunny hills in the distance: they all look like images thrown down to earth through a prism—translucent, weightless, composed of pure light. You could carry it all with you on your back, or it could all just blow away.

I'm having this insight into the nature of things when I see my first butterfly of the year, a big monarch floating down through the telephone wires in front of Mom's store.

Maybe it's my first butterfly in many years; I can't remember the last time I saw one. We don't get butterflies in my part of Brooklyn. The monarch wobbles over my head, and when I spin around I see it land next to a cluster of four or five more on the ledge beneath Mom's plate-glass window. I hear a tap on the glass; in her space behind the cash register, Mom is fluttering her fingers like butterflies and smiling at me. I nod and point to them on her ledge and kneel down on the sidewalk next to the newspaper rack.

They're all big ones, clinging together, opening and closing themselves as if breathing with their wings. In the sunlight you can almost see right through them. They don't mind being scrutinized, but when I put out a finger to stroke one of their wings they all leap off the glass and swirl around my head. I leap up and swirl around too, shooing them out of my eyes, and then everybody except me flies away. In Mom's storefront window I can see my reflection —the startled expression on my face, the butterflies and red trees in the blue sky behind me—and beneath that, Mom herself, shaking her head at me and laughing.

It was Guy and Vita who introduced me to June, almost six years ago now. If I'd been more serious about having a career I might have met her on my own, without anybody's help. She was a grad student in journalism here like the rest of us—Guy in photography, Vita and June in newspaper, me in magazine. I'd been seeing her around. Sooner or later, I figured, I'd have a chance to get her attention. But I wasn't on campus a month when I bailed right out of that journalism school.

You could say the curriculum was Mickey Mouse, but it was more than that. It was the Darwinian version of Disneyland, where the cartoons eat each other. In one class, the professor clipped articles from magazines he didn't like, made us rewrite them to a formula he'd devised, and then ridiculed, in public, the departures from his system. Another guy gave a proofreading test the first day and then announced individual failings at the second class. "I see that Mr. Jenson cannot distinguish the run-on paragraph." Three weeks into the term they had a bunch of nice people ready to knife each other for a scrap of praise.

I went to see my graduate adviser, a man who'd run a business monthly for years before hanging up his editing pen. He was chairman of the magazine department. I told him how I felt. He nodded sympathetically and slapped his pipe against the palm of his hand. Then he suggested I leave the program.

"You don't need us, Adam," he said, tamping new tobacco into his bowl. "If you really want a career in journalism, nothing will stop you. Human determination is like water on rock, son. That's why I discourage as many as I can. It's best when only the toughest get through. That way, if a magazine buys product from this department, it'll be good product, and they'll buy again."

I thanked the man and got up to leave, but he motioned me back to my chair. He lit his pipe, and the fruity blue smoke hung between us like a veil. It didn't work out for me in journalism, he said, but that didn't mean I had to leave grad school altogether. After all, I was here already. He'd be glad to make a call for me. Was there something else I'd care to study?

In college I'd been an English major. I said it might be nice to read literature some more.

"No, not that," he said right away. "Anything but that. What would you write about? Writing?" He smiled smugly, then leaned toward me through the haze. "Have you ever considered philosophy?" he asked.

The high-mindedness of his suggestion took me by surprise. In fact, I'd always been interested in philosophy, and I told him so. He nodded approvingly. His approbation and the clubby atmosphere of his smoke relaxed me. I sat back in my chair to accept the massage of good guidance, warm and hopeful sensations about the next phase of my life running through me like soothing fingers. Why philosophy? I asked my soon-to-be ex-adviser.

"I've just read a fascinating study," he said, a fragrant cloud issuing from his face. "It turns out that more rich widows marry philosophy professors than men from any other group."

They were happy to have me over in English. My new adviser gloated over snatching a young life away from the press. I read Jonathan Swift all day and nobody bothered me. But I never saw the intriguing June, whose schedule did not involve the Humanities building. I had, however, become friends with Guy. His girlfriend, Vita, knew June quite well. Later that semester they invited us both to dinner.

And that was that. June finished her degree, and we moved down to New York where she had an offer from one of the wire services. I found a writing job with a giant financial institution which is either saving the world or destroying it, depending upon your perspective. I compose their brochures and I pick up my check. Guy and Vita never left town at all. She went to work for the city's arts weekly; to no one's surprise, she runs the thing today. Guy figured out that he took pictures because he liked the way they looked, not because he liked covering the news, and he dropped out of the J-school too. Later he found a nice little niche for himself up here: photo curator at the university archives.

They ended up buying the very house they rented back then, and that's why we're here this week—we're returning to the scene. For me, the old days are getting as ghostly now as the daguerreotypes Guy looks after, pictures that would fade away forever if he didn't know how to preserve them or make a decent copy. Already I don't remember many things that people tell me happened back then. But some shots in my album have remained clear and bright— only, it seems, so I could return them to the photographer, put them back in the camera.

We've been on relationship probation, June and I. Six months of it now.

It makes some of my vivid pictures wicked to conjure up: me, for example, predicting to June, the week we started out, that she and I would never fight. And her: hooting and rolling her eyes. Or this later one, five years and a million fights later, after a real out-and-out clash of the titans: June standing before me in our tiny place in New York, weeping and giving us one last chance—six months to prove we could live together in peace.

So how have we done? Pretty well, if anybody's asking me, though I'm not sure anybody is. Yes, we have fought during our probation, many times, but those fights don't count, I maintain, because they weren't real fights. We always wore the big gloves and the face masks and kept the concept of probation uppermost in our minds. When we clinched against the ropes, our probation leapt between us like a ref.

We have not gone at each other like doomsday, the way we used to do. We have shown restraint. My personal opinion is that we've come through OK.

But I don't know how June feels about it. She has refused, the whole time, to preview the state of her mind— refused even to express any desire that things go one way or the other. So I don't know what she's decided. But I will before long. Our probation was six months to the day, and today's the day.

And this was June's idea too—spending our last probation weekend in the house where we met. "Doesn't that strike you as an elegant thing?" she said a few weeks ago. "We could confront our old selves, all our old demons. We'd have the nice feeling of not running away from anything."

"Running away could be a brilliant strategy," I said. "For all you know, the demons are counting on you to get brave and make it easy for them. Remember that old saying? 'The early worm gets eaten by the bird.'"

"A worm invented that," June replied.

On Guy's front porch now I can hear music playing on the stereo inside—the *Eric Dolphy Memorial Album,* the record we left on the turntable last night. Guy has been on an Eric Dolphy jag this weekend, no complaints from me. I open the door, and the music becomes a loud, warm color in the air of the house. I'm crossing the threshold when I

see another cluster of monarchs clinging to the porch railing—big as the ones at Mom's, huddled together, fantastic
eyes staring back at me from their wings. I don't try to
touch them this time. In the kitchen, Guy is wearing a
barbecue apron over his bathrobe and mincing cilantro and
tomatoes for the salsa. I lean over the cutting board for a
sniff, Dolphy's pungent saxophone like a sound track for
the tangy fumes rising into my face. Guy takes a big sniff,
too, and covers his eyes with his free hand.

"She's coming into focus," he says. "The woman in the
dream. She's tall. She moves like a dancer but she's too tall
for ballet. Whoops, now she's starting to fade. Quick, grape
boy. Lay those grapes on me."

June and Vita were showing no signs of getting out of bed,
so Guy cranked up the music until they emerged sleepy-
eyed in their robes, grumbling about the pestilence known
as men. Now we have Dolphy's *Iron Man* simmering on
the stereo at a sociable volume. We're all together at the
dining room table having Guy's breakfast invention and
discussing his dream. The food looks ridiculous, but it
tastes surprisingly good.

"The most important thing," Vita says, "is that Guy
never saw her face. That's pretty revealing, Guy. That says
so much. She didn't have a face."

Since the last time we were here, Vita has shorn her long
head of hair, and the new haircut makes her look a lot like
Jean Seberg in the original *Breathless*, though Vita's hair is
black and Seberg's wasn't.

"She might have had a face," Guy says, "and I just didn't see it."

"No, no," Vita says. "What you see is what you get. Especially in dreams."

"You didn't see her eat her eggs," I say. "That could be significant."

"I was wrapped up in my own," Guy says. "She might have eaten hers without my noticing."

"Her eggs," Vita says to June. "Do you believe this dream?"

June considers this while finishing a bite of food. "I think the key thing is that Guy responded creatively to the presence of this unknown woman." She holds up a forkful of grapes and eggs. "He invented this delicious new breakfast for her."

"But she demanded it," I say. "She showed up in his kitchen making demands, insisting on something completely new to eat."

"Of course that was Guy making demands on himself," June says.

"I don't know about that," Guy says. "She felt pretty real. Maybe sometimes a woman is just a woman."

"I think it was your feminine, creative nature," June says.

"Oh, I'm glad you mentioned that," Guy says. He goes out to the living room and comes back with a handful of Eric Dolphy album covers. "We want to get your feminine, creative opinions about something." He hands each of them a few record jackets.

Dolphy, who's been dead for more than twenty years, had a large, peculiar lump on his forehead. I've always thought of it as an egg about to burst out of his head and hatch. In every picture of him I've ever seen, the lump is perched up there, off center, above his left eye. We were talking about it late last night, after the women went to bed. Guy has the idea that the lump was what killed Dolphy, that it was a tumor of some kind. He thinks that Dolphy was carrying his own death around on his head, and that his blowing so hard on his horns finally forced it to break free and enter his blood. I don't buy it. In their time as journalists, Vita and June have covered many medical stories, hung around hospitals, interviewed doctors and nurses. We said we'd abide by their judgment. It's an old idea, really—that what you love is what finally kills you—and I think we're both hoping that it won't be true.

Vita sips her coffee and compares a few views of Dolphy's head. "It's nothing," she says finally.

"What a relief," I say.

"How could it be nothing?" Guy says. "A huge lump on the man's head."

"Well, nothing fatal," Vita says. "Some kind of fatty cyst, benign beyond a doubt. Nothing. It didn't kill him."

"If it could have killed him," June says, "he would have known about it. He would have seen doctors and had it attended to."

"Saxophone players are not famous for their regular medical checkups," Guy says. "God bless them."

"Guy," June says, "it was a fairly, you know, *apparent* thing."

"The verdict's in," I say. "Playing jazz is not hazardous to your health."

"I think his intensity got him," Guy says. "You can hear how intense he was."

There's no quarrel about the intensity. On the stereo now Dolphy is playing Ellington's "Come Sunday" on bass clarinet, and he sounds like a great woolly mastodon going extinct right there in the living room.

"I don't suppose either of you care how he actually died," June says.

"The two journalism dropouts," Vita says.

"As a matter of fact, we don't," I say.

"We're the type of men who search for things to believe in," Guy says. "Big things, unfettered by mere actuality."

"Anybody can believe in actuality," I say, and I look out the front window for a glimpse of something actual to use as an example. About a dozen huge monarchs are clinging to the glass. "The butterflies around here are incredible," I say. "Big clusters of them all over the place."

"Monarch butterflies," June says without looking.

"Right. Why, is this a special year for them or something? Like locusts? I've seen about thirty this morning alone."

"They stop here this time every year," June says. "You really don't know about them? They're a famous thing about this town. They're on their way south. They migrate to California and Mexico."

"Butterflies don't migrate, June," I say.

"Monarchs migrate," she says.

"He doesn't know about the butterflies," Guy says.

"Not only do they migrate," June says, "they stop in exactly the same places every year, just the way birds do, and one of those places is that huge cemetery on the other side of campus."

"You were excited about seeing thirty of them?" Vita says. "There's probably a million out there right now."

"Don't you read the paper?" Guy says. "There was an article about it yesterday. This is the peak butterfly weekend. Scientists are here from all over the world."

"I saw it once," June says. "With the guy I was seeing before you, in fact. It was unbelievable."

"We go every year," Vita says. "But with you two using our house as a love hospice, I forgot all about it."

"You've never seen my butterfly pictures?" Guy says.

"You think it's fall foliage on the trees," June says, "but it's *butterflies*. I can't believe you didn't know about them. It's just your kind of thing."

"You didn't do much entomology while you were here," Guy says.

"I wasn't here to do entomology," I say.

"Oh, right, I forgot," he says. "You were here to meet girls."

Photographs from various points in Guy's career are hanging all over his house, but in the guest room downstairs there's only one, on the wall across from the bed. It's a picture of Vita's hands—a large black-and-white print, bright woman's hands floating in a voidlike darkness. Her left hand is nestled in her right, the long fingers tapering to short, clear, nicely shaped nails. A row of small moonstones shines on the only ring she wears, a ring Guy bought for her when they went to Italy.

That's all there is to it. That and the things you can't really talk about: the way the hands *announce* themselves in the picture, and the way Guy has *descended* upon them with his camera—swooped down upon Vita's hands like the great god-bird possessing the girl.

I've been contemplating this picture since we arrived two days ago. If it was hanging here last year, the last time we stayed in this house, I must have been walking around in my sleep. That's possible; it wouldn't have been the first time. But I'm almost certain the picture is new to the guest-room wall.

And that it's been placed there for me. That's the way Guy would do it.

Two nights in a row, I've sat up in bed looking at the picture while June read magazines beside me. You might think people in our situation would be talking feverishly now—proposing and counter-proposing, making demands and last-minute appeals—but June calls our relationship "that old R-Factor," and she won't discuss it anymore. The time for talk is gone, she says, and I have to agree. It's time now for June to feel her way into that zone of all possible futures—the place where everything that could happen and every person you might possibly become are arrayed before you in a kind of sculpture garden of the soul, and you wander around at your leisure comparing the dwarves and the gnomes. Everybody gets to choose one future-sculpture to call his or her own, and June will do that. She will take all the time she has coming to her, and then she will make up her mind.

Right now she's upstairs taking a bubble bath. When she's done with that we're going out to meet Guy on cam-

pus, where he has gone to assemble his camera gear. Then
we're all going to the cemetery together.

In the meantime I'm looking at Vita's actual hands, the
ones on her body, from across the living room sofa I'm
sharing with her. In life they're larger than they seem in
the picture, and they're flipping, at this moment, through
one of Guy's photography magazines while their owner
makes snorting and grunting sounds. Finally she asks,
"Why do I have the feeling that all these photographers
are men?"

She turns the magazine around and holds it open so I
can see a picture of a model standing on a beach in a bright
red bathing suit. The bathing suit is a single V-shaped strip
of cloth that runs from the woman's crotch to her shoulders in one red flash, barely covering her various parts on
the way. For some reason she's wearing a pair of electric-
blue running shoes, and in this picture she's looking down
at the shoes and laughing because the surf is splashing over
her feet. She seems good-natured to me, someone who en-
joys a joke at her own expense. I feel drawn to the model in
the picture; I think I'd like her if I met her in person.

"She's out running," Vita says. "What do you suppose
she's running from?"

"From her agent," I say. "Her agent wants her to do a
laundry soap commercial where a washing machine starts
talking to her, and she's afraid of machines that talk."

"Aren't we all," Vita says. "Do you like her suit? Would
you like a girlfriend in a bathing suit like that?"

"Part of my brain might like it," I say.

"The reptilian part," she says, and even she has to laugh.

"Right," I say. "When the feminist surgeons take the lid

off my head, that's what they'll find, a big iguana flicking out his tongue at bathing suits."

"It would be nice if there *was* an iguana in there," Vita says. "That way they could just take that part out." She smiles with her lips closed tight. "There *are* feminist surgeons, by the way."

"I knew that," I say.

"What's this about feminist surgeons?" June says, bouncing down the stairs all pink from her bath. She's wearing a white sweatshirt with big Chinese characters printed on it, the sleeves and throat cut away, and blousy green pants tied off at the ankles with strings.

"We were discussing some modifications to Mr. Butterfly here," Vita says.

"I've researched that subject," June says. "But I never got as far as putting him under the knife."

"They can do amazing things these days," Vita says.

"They can go in and clip your circuits," I say. "I read an article about this guy they did it to. But it was a failure. When he got home, his left hand tried to kill his wife while his right hand tried to save her."

"They just made him normal," Vita says.

"They can do other things, too. They can poke electrodes in there and make people laugh when they're not really happy."

"That might be indicated in your case," June says.

"He tugged at his leash when he saw this," Vita says, handing June the opened photography magazine.

June whistles when she sees the picture. "Nice. Just the way we used to look, right?" she says to Vita, and grabs a

handful of hip. "He was recently telling me that I'm getting broad in the beam."

"That was a joke," I say.

"Better get him to the doc right away," Vita says, "before he starts making appointments for you."

I get up off the sofa and slap my thighs, a jolly fellow.
"So what's our strategy on these butterflies?" I say.

"Yeah, what's our strategy?" Vita says. "We have to have
a strategy, right? Are we going to go out there and act real
amazed, and let a million butterflies know they knock us
out? Let on that we love them to pieces? Or are we going
to be coy about it?"

"Oh, coy for sure," June says. "Coy supreme. We'll hide
behind a tombstone."

Guy the archivist works in a lab in the new library complex,
but Guy the artist has his own office at the campus dark-
rooms in the student union building. He's sitting behind
his desk there now, twisting lenses onto his cameras and
loading them with film. June and Vita are off buying each
other presents at the college store, which is open this Sunday because it turns out to be, of all the humiliating things,
Homecoming Weekend.

"Did you know that when you planned this trip?" I
asked June, but she hadn't known. We discovered it at the
same instant—when we drove onto campus just now with
Vita and found the place looking like Sportswear World.
Vita meant to tell us and forgot. She thinks it's funny.
"They didn't know you were coming, either," she said.
"It's on account of the butterflies. Some booster in the

Alumni Office got that idea a few years ago—make Home-coming coincide with the famous monarch stopover. Get it?"

"We get it," June said.

"I hold no degree from this institution," I said. "I'm off the books here."

"How do people from Alumni Offices find each other?" June wanted to know.

"They go to school together," Vita said.

Guy's darkroom office is plastered with photographs, some of them carefully matted and framed, most merely pushpinned to the walls. I walk around looking while I wait for him, and after a minute I begin to recognize people. There's a portrait of the two hippie couples who ran the health food store; June and I shopped with them until they left town to join a collective farm in Tennessee. The farm had its own communal religion in which every member married every other member in mammoth wedding cere-monies. Their leader placed great emphasis on going forth and multiplying; if you were a man you dealt babies to the group like cards in a poker game. Farther along the wall I see an English professor I studied with, a woman adored by her students. She was denied tenure while I was taking her course, in a wave of tenure denials known on campus that year as the Purge of the Cool People. I heard she finally left teaching altogether to take up jazz piano. And there are numerous pictures of Vita when her hair was long, and of other people when their hair was long, too—old friends of Guy's, I guess, frozen in their youth next to Volkswagen vans and organic gardens.

Guy finishes setting up his gear. "I made some things for you," he says, leading me down the hall.

Only the red safety lamps are on in his darkroom. In the weird light, Guy's tangerine shirt is gray, and everything else is some other wrong color. It makes you think you're in a movie—the scene from *Blow-Up,* say, where David Hemmings finally figures things out—or deep down inside a mummy's tomb.

Guy jostles some plastic trays full of fluid next to the sink. "I think we're just about fixed here," he says, lifting a wet picture from one of the trays and clipping it to a wire strung beneath the cabinets on the wall. "This is called stopping a picture—putting it in a fixative bath like this. It makes the printing process stop. They did the same thing in the old days, but the chemicals are a lot better now."

He hangs up another dripping picture. They don't look like anything to me—a jumble of gray shapes in the spectral light.

"As a matter of fact, that's why I have the job I have," Guy says. "Did you know that? In the old days, people fixed pictures with stuff that eventually makes them self-destruct. The pictures, I mean. The old prints I work on in the archives are literally eating themselves." He attaches a third print to the wire and then he flips on the overhead lights. Everything becomes normal again. "I still don't know how you managed to miss these things," he says.

I step to the counter and look. In the first picture, thousands of monarch butterflies are clinging to the limb of a tree. Their wings are folded up and they're packed so close together that they look like spiky fur on the leg of some great black-and-orange beast. It's extreme behavior, not something an entire life form would do on a whim.

"They all want to be on specific butterfly trees," Guy says while I stare at the picture. "But get this. They're the descendants of the ones from the previous year. They've never been to this cemetery before, yet they land in the very same trees their great-great-grandparents landed in. They've never been anywhere near Mexico either, but when they get down there they fly right to the proper butterfly place and land on the proper butterfly trees. Nobody knows how they do it."

We sidle along the countertop. The second picture is of a massive stone mausoleum overshadowed by a giant tree, and the third is the wrought-iron entrance gate of the cemetery. Everything in the pictures is covered with butterflies —great patches of them like black-and-orange blankets, or ropy trails like Hawaiian leis.

Guy reaches into the last fixing tray and hangs up one more soaking print. "What's wrong with this picture?" he says, smiling and quite pleased with himself.

It's a picture of a man and a woman. Her I recognize instantly, and the first thing I feel is amusing—a little blip of fear that I won't know the man she's with. Then I recognize him too. It's me, sitting some years ago with June in a folding lounge chair on the edge of some woods, smiling for the camera like the happiest guy in the world. We were at a big picnic by a lake not far from here, a great picnic with just about everybody we knew. I'd forgotten all about that day, but now I remember it as one of the best times I ever had. I hold a loose corner of the picture to look at it. June is smiling too, a gorgeous smile, and I have to laugh at the next things I feel: that I'd like to meet this alluring woman who looks like someone I could never imagine finding anything to fight about with.

"Can I remind you of something?" I say to Guy.

"Sure."

"You're the one who dreams of beautiful women who come to your home looking for nourishment they've never had."

He puts his arm around my shoulders. "The woman in the dream is easy," he says. "She knew there was a guy in my house who was always dishing out the same old chow. She entered my head by mistake. She was really looking for you."

We're driving to the cemetery in Vita's Volvo, Guy at the wheel, me in the passenger seat. The women are in the back, singing along with a new cassette June bought for Vita at the campus bookstore. They're playing the tape on Vita's walkaround cassette machine with two sets of micro-headphones coming out of it, so in the front we can't hear the music itself, just their singing along. It sounds spooky between choruses when suddenly they fall silent for a while and then just as suddenly begin singing again. At one point there must be a long instrumental section because they both start making different kinds of random humming sounds—sax solos and guitar breaks that don't fit together very well. They can't hear each other either, I remind myself. Vita bought June a pair of beach-punky silvered sunglasses and a straw sun hat, and she's wearing those. It's bright and sunny out.

Guy winks at me. "The campfire girls at century's end," he says. "Singing their way into your heart."

We reach the cemetery, and as we drive beneath the entrance gate I see that it is indeed covered with monarch butterflies—not so many as in Guy's picture but an amazing number nonetheless, woven through the green ivy that climbs the black wrought iron. He parks the car in a cul-de-sac full of fallen leaves. I help him unload his equipment from the trunk while the women take off their headphones and stow the tape player in there. June catches my eye, then tugs me away from the car by my ear. "I've made up my mind," she whispers. "I'll tell you when we get back." Then she and Vita go running across the lawn, holding hands and laughing. Guy hangs his cameras around his neck and puts his silver tripod over my shoulder like a rifle. "Be a good soldier," he says.

And here I must be forgiven an impertinence—it certainly is one—but for a second I know the feeling of the prisoner taken into the woods by captors who insist they only want to show him the beautiful countryside.

We walk across an empty stretch of lawn and into the first range of tombstones. This is a vast memorial park with as many trees as an arboretum and an enormous number of graves. It's an astonishing thing, how many people have died. The graves in this section are very old—Civil War vintage or earlier, with the waferlike headstones they made by hand back then. Most of the old stones have tilted backward over the years so that the rain hits their faces, and now their inscriptions are virtually gone.

Guy is walking among these blank stones, looking up into the trees. "I was talking to this bug guy at school last week," he says. "You know what the monarchs get to eat between here and Mexico? Almost nothing. They store up as much fat as they can in their bodies and somehow they make it on that. Nobody can understand it. It's one of the great mysteries."

He stops and puts his toe on the grass, and I see that he's pointing with his sneaker to a dead monarch lying there with half a wing gone. It's about as big as the ones I saw at Mom's—as fattened up as they get for the long flight, except this one isn't going.

"The birds go after them," Guy says.

And then I see that dead monarchs are lying all over the ground, whole ones and torn ones mingled with the fallen leaves.

"Some monarchs are good to eat," Guy says, kneeling to take a picture of one. "But many of them will make a bird sick. It depends on what kind of milkweed they've been feeding on. That used to be their protection, that birds would associate them with being sick. But then the hungry birds figured out that some monarchs are perfectly OK, and they learned to tell which is which on first taste. Now they just drop the bad ones."

June and Vita have climbed to the top of a knoll covered by elaborate monuments and memorial statuary. They're sitting on the grass up there in the orange light filtering down through a gigantic tree. I start to head that way, but Guy turns onto a path that leads to an evergreen grove at the edge of the cemetery. He stops on the path and takes one long shot of the grove; then he walks in and crouches down to photograph a particular stone. When I reach him, he nods for me to look. It's a man with a long Italian name who died several years ago. The stone gives the name of the Italian town where he was born. Fresh flowers are on his grave.

"Pop," I say.

"Right," Guy says. "Pop. I stopped in there on my way to school today and she asked me about my bad friend who likes the butterflies. When I told her we were coming here, she asked for a picture of him while these flowers were fresh. I've done it for her before, but it was in the winter when there was snow all over him." He takes a few more shots of Pop's grave.

"She thinks I'm married to June," I say.

Guy smiles and nods his head. "I know. She thinks I'm married to Vita."

We walk out of the grove, back into the sun. Butterflies are swooping through the air in clusters of a dozen or so. Here and there, groups of people are wandering along. I wonder if they came just to pay their respects, and what they think of the monarch migration. If you didn't know what it was, it could frighten you, like some kind of pestilence called down on your ancestors.

Up on the knoll, Vita is clambering onto an equestrian monument with a boost from her old friend June. Finally she's sitting on the horse's rump with her arms around the dead man's waist. He was a cavalryman, and his sword is raised in the air for the charge. Vita waves to us and we wave back, and Guy takes her picture with a telephoto lens. It must be uncomfortable up there because soon she climbs down and starts chasing June around the big tree.

"They like each other," I say.

"They're likable people," Guy says. "Could be showing a bit more respect for the dead, however."

"I don't remember Vita as so much fun and games," I say.

Guy watches her in the distance. "She used to be more severe," he says. "More strident." He laughs. "Abrasive, actually."

"I never thought I'd really get to know her."

"Well, you didn't like her," he says. "That's OK. She didn't like you either. But she says she likes you better now. In fact, she's a fan of yours. She says she's rooting for you, champ. In the big showdown here."

When we get to the top of the knoll, the women are sitting arm in arm beneath the tree. Dead butterflies are lying all over the ground, but there are leaves all over the ground too, and when I look up I see that it's not simply fall foliage making the light look orange; half the leaves have already fallen. The tree is possessed by monarchs—countless thousands of them all over it, the way the kudzu vine will take over a tree down south.

"If I'd known about this in the old days, I would have camped out here to be with it," I say. "I might have stayed for a Ph.D. if I'd known. I might have made my life here like the two of you. Who *wouldn't* come to see this?"

"I'm sure plenty of people born and raised in this town have never been up here to see it," June says.

"There are people born and raised in this town," Vita says, "who don't even know there's a university here."

"You're right," I say. "I always forget about them."

Guy takes the tripod from my shoulder and sets it up on

the grass. "I'm hungry now," he says. "We should have brought a picnic."

"The butterfly king is making dinner for us later," Vita says. "Then he's going back to his kingdom tomorrow to reign with his queen."

I look at June, mysterious in her hat-and-sunglasses disguise. "Is that what the queen says?" I say.

June smiles and waves to me. "That's what she says," she says. Then she slips her leg between my legs and pulls until I fall down on the leaves and butterfly bodies.

"Long live the butterfly king and queen," says Guy. "What are you making us for dinner?"

"I'm thinking about fettuccine with a butterfly-and-wine sauce," I say. "A recipe for it just came to me."

"Now this is fascinating," Vita says. "The men are starting to cook with their primal, mythic brains. Maybe their food will have special healing powers."

"Let's hope so," June says.

Guy takes a few pictures of the tree, and then he fastens one of his cameras to the tripod. "It's group picture time," he says.

"Yay," Vita says, and she and June get off the ground, hauling me up between them. They put their arms around my shoulders, and I put my arms around theirs.

"We need a butterfly branch," Guy says, walking backward with the tripod.

"What about you?" June asks.

"I'll be in it," he says. "I'm putting it on automatic."

He sets it up, and then he hustles over to stand on the end of our chain with his arm around Vita's waist. We all get smiles on our faces. But then just as we're ready, a flock

of crows comes swooping into our tree to attack the butterflies, and the butterflies burst into the air like a sandstorm.
The crows screech like demons and chase their prey, and
their prey goes crazy, swarming all through the air around
us. We're hunched over and twirling around, covering our
eyes and swiping butterflies away from our heads. And in
the middle of all this, I hear Guy's camera go off, but the
cloud of monarchs is so dense I can't even see the tripod.
When the picture comes out it'll be amazing, but you
won't even know we were there.

MEN UNDER WATER

The Peter Pan Diner, 10:30 A.M. Breakfast with
Gunther.

"You're depressed again," Gunther says to me. "I can
tell." He has the catsup bottle in one fist like a chisel or a
caulking gun, and with the heel of his other hand he's
hammering catsup over his hash browns and scrambled
eggs. He's getting some on the bacon and toast, too.

"I'm not depressed," I say.

"You're not eating."

"Gunther, I eat at home, remember? At breakfast time.
I never eat here."

He slips into his pouting voice. "You used to," he says.

This is a bad sign. It means that Gunther is especially
needy and delusional today. I haven't ordered anything but

coffee in the Peter Pan since the first week I worked for him, more than six months ago.

I look at him, busying himself with breakfast on the other side of the booth. Lately I've spent more hours of each week with Gunther than I've spent with my wife, and still there are times—this moment is one of them—when I see him as I saw him the day we met, times when I cannot get beyond the amazing epidermal surface of the man. Gunther is one of the largest people I've ever known, but it's more than that, more than his general enormousness, the smooth expanse of his completely bald head, the perfect beardlessness of his broad face. Gunther has no eyebrows, no body hair whatsoever as far as I know; even the large nostrils of his great, wide nose are pink hairless tunnels running up into his skull. His velour pullover is open to his sternum, and the exposed chest is precisely the complexion of all the rest of him—the shrimplike color of new Play-Doh, the substance from which Gunther sometimes seems to be made. Under the movie lights he likes to muck around with, his skin goes translucent and you can watch the blood vessels keeping him alive.

"If you're not depressed," he says around a mouthful of catsup and eggs, "what are you?"

"Subdued," I say.

"Oh," he says. "Well, would you mind knocking off being subdued? You're not putting out any energy. I can't do it all by myself."

"Do what?"

"Write this goddam screenplay," he says.

"Oh. Which screenplay is this?"

"You know perfectly well which screenplay. The sci-fi

one with the giant radioactive crayfish and the girl scientist who understands them, and who's also the love interest for the guy scientist. The one we've been working on all week."

"Oh, that one," I say. "I forgot. I thought maybe you meant the Kung Fu screenplay. I guess that was last week."

"You want to work on that one? Hey, we could even do a hybrid of the two. Say these huge radioactive crayfish attack mankind with a sort of lobster version of Kung Fu, bopping people with their big claws. The guy scientist also happens to be a martial-arts master. In the end, he conquers the lobsters by building robots programmed to hit them in their pressure points. But before that there's a scene where the lobsters grab the girl and he has to take a couple of them down with his bare hands."

"No, Gunther." I sip my coffee and stare out the window above the personal jukebox mounted on the wall of our booth. The jukebox is playing Roy Orbison's "Pretty Woman," Gunther's favorite song. He put it on to cheer me up.

Outside, a light gray ash is falling from the sky like rain. Cleveland has a lot of smokestack industry, and the Peter Pan is one of the venerable old smokestack-area diners. That's why we come here to eat. Not because we work in the plants ourselves—our work, like God, is everywhere and nowhere—but because this is where reality is, the life and labor of the folk, the source of all art. Someday, after he's made the two or three commercial pictures that will establish him as one of the major film forces of our time, Gunther wants to celebrate his native city in a cinematic tone poem about the ballet of heavy manufacture, the romance of rubber and steel.

I show him my wristwatch. "What about the Puerto Rican couple on Liberty Place with the gas leak in their stove? Or the nursing students on Meadow with no hot water? You told them today for sure. And your answering service. I'll bet you didn't call your answering service. You'll call it at three this afternoon, and then we'll have to work until nine tonight."

Gunther throws his fork onto his plate. People at the counter turn on their stools to look at us. "This is your whole problem," he says. He clangs his coffee cup with his spoon to get the attention of our waitress. It's Alice today, a good woman. If Gunther gets too abusive, she'll pour coffee in his lap. She's done it before. She comes over now and fills our cups.

"I try to foster a creative spirit," Gunther says to me. Alice flashes him a look, the coffeepot poised in the air. He stops talking and stares at the table until she's gone on her way. "I try to pay you for your imagination," he says, "not just for dumb monkey work I could get anybody to do. I try to treat you like an artist. And all you want to do is fix toilets." He picks up the cream and sugar and pours long streams of each into his cup. Then he starts the singsongy voice. "Yes, for a certain number of hours each week we have to do some essentially noncreative work, things that are not really what artists like us should be doing—painting apartments, replacing water heaters, fixing toilets. But it keeps us humble, I say. I try to be philosophical about it. I don't go into a mood just because I can't work on my movies every minute of every day."

"I left my house three hours ago, Gunther."

"Here we go again," he says.

He doesn't start paying my hourly wages until we leave the diner. But if I don't go over to Gunther's house each morning and wake him up and, while he takes a shower, watch parts of movies he's videotaped, and then listen to him rant about screenplays over breakfast at the Peter Pan, we won't go to work at all and I won't be paid anything.

He turns to the jukebox and speaks to Roy Orbison. "Roy," he says, "what am I going to do with this guy? Sensitive and gifted, yes, but he has real limitations. He actually wants to work for wages." He turns back to me. "You're not being flexible," he says. "That's a major character flaw; you should watch that. How many times have I explained this to you? You're working for—and will soon be the partner of—an important motion picture producer who happens at the moment to be trapped inside a landlord's body."

"That's not how it was advertised," I say. "It was advertised: 'Handyman and general helper, no experience necessary.' That's the ad I responded to. You changed it to scriptwriter after I was hired."

"After I discovered the talent I can't let you throw away, even if you want to. A good part of each week is ours to be talented together, you and me. We toss some ideas back and forth"—he slaps my shoulder—"and in a couple of weeks we have a screenplay. I round up some investors, we start shooting the movie, we're on our way. We could have made some progress on this movie right here at breakfast, but no, you're subdued. You think that just because we

have to go fix a toilet today, that's all we are, two guys who
have to fix a toilet, and you let it get you down."

"What toilet?" I say. "You're keeping something from
me."

"Weren't you the one who wanted me to call my answering service?"

He stands up and tosses his wadded napkin onto his
plate, smiling and bobbing his head from side to side like
Hardy to Laurel. He leans toward me over the table as if to
confide a great truth, a truth that will be true long after
everything else is dust. "Rock band," he says, and strides
away from the booth. Then he comes back, doing his
wicked leer. "The horror, the horror," he adds.

We pay our bill and stroll out of the Peter Pan into the
sunlight and ashes, me in my paint-spattered carpenter's
pants and sweatshirt, Gunther swaggering in his red-and-
yellow-striped velour pullover and racing shades. It's 11:30
A.M., almost time for lunch. The rest of the world has
already accomplished much since waking, and laid down
foundations for the accomplishment of much more. We
have accomplished nothing. But neither have we yet lost
everything, I remind myself. We still have much of what
we had when the day began. I have my job with Gunther—
twenty dollars an hour under the table, starting now—and
Gunther has his small real estate empire, his Ford Bronco,
the ability to pay me twenty dollars for each hour I ride
around in it with him, and an unflagging, magical belief in
the rightness of his life and methods despite all evidence to
the contrary.

And he has me. We have each other.

. ■ .

Tina, my wife, cannot believe I continue to hold this job. We need the money, but Tina has had enough. She can't take any more stories about Gunther. She can't take what working for Gunther is doing to me. I'm no longer the man she married, Tina says. My inability to leave Gunther has raised serious questions about the deep structure of my personality, and now Tina wants us both to go in for counseling. She says she's become a kind of co-alcoholic, living through my experiences with this man. She's had to go through it all with me, even though it's not her life, and now in some perverse way she feels that she works for Gunther too.

Every night when I get home I must drink for one full hour and rail to Tina about Gunther. I tell her what Gunther has done to me that day, what he's done to his tenants, the lies he's made me tell the tenants about those things, the movie-script ideas he's forced me to invent. After an hour I'm usually able to take a shower and have dinner. But it's growing longer now, up to two hours sometimes. At first it was exotic and Tina enjoyed it. Every night I would bring home amazing new stories. Tina would listen and shake her head in wonder, marveling over the character of Gunther, the shamelessness of the business world, the length and breadth of the illusions men can entertain about themselves.

But then late last winter I came home one night with the Pakistani-baby story. Tina teaches in a day-care center, and the Pakistani-baby story pushed her over the edge. I'd been shoveling snow at Gunther's garden-apartment buildings when a Pakistani woman came out into the parking lot in her flowing ocher robes, weeping and screaming because there was no heat and her baby was freezing. I went inside to have a look, something I'm not supposed to do on my own. I'm supposed to refer tenants to Gunther's answering service, nothing more. In the apartment I could see my breath more clearly than I could outside. The woman's baby was swaddled in many blankets; only its nose and lips were sticking out, and they were blue. Sitting at the dinette table in his overcoat was the woman's husband, a little brown man with mournful eyes, eating a bowl of curry and shivering. Something big snapped inside me when I saw their lives. I showed them how to call the tenants'-rights division of Legal Aid, and then I gave them Gunther's unlisted home number, the most forbidden thing there is. Gunther and I had our biggest fight over the Pakistani family. When I got home, Tina spent the whole evening trying to calm me down. I quit for two entire weeks that time, finally going back for three dollars more an hour.

But now I must quit this job forever, Tina says—really quit, not just quit the way I do every week.

Every Friday when Gunther pays me what I'm owed, I put the cash in my pocket and say Sayonara. After a full week of Gunther, I can't envision one more day. He shakes his head, looks at the ground, asks me what he's done wrong. Nothing, Gunther, I always say, not a thing, you're a prince. I just can't take the real estate life anymore.

You lack vision, he always says. You're turning your back on a brilliant future. The real estate is only a stop along the way, Reggie. Next stop, Hollywood!

No can do, Gunther, I say. We shake hands and go our

separate ways forever. Sunday morning I buy the paper and read the ads. Again each week, in return for two thirds of a person's waking life, the free market offers enough money to rent a shed and eat a can of beans every day. "I'm presently holding the best job in Cleveland," I tell Tina. She puts her hands over her ears. Then Sunday afternoon Gunther calls to offer me an hourly increase of fifty cents over what I made the previous week. I accept his new offer. I started at four dollars an hour. I'm up to twenty now. In his big house on a hill above town, Gunther has shown me where he hides his gun. When I reach fifty dollars an hour, he wants me to kill him.

Gunther's real estate holdings consist of two three-story brick garden-apartment buildings down near the Projects, eight or nine rambling wooden Victorians scattered all over the rest of town, and miscellaneous. Miscellaneous includes some garages Gunther rents to people for their cars, and a couple of apartments he has the nerve to rent over the garages. Of the enormous Victorians, three are divided vertically into two-families, and another five or six—the ones in the better areas—have been partitioned into warrens of small studios and one-bedrooms for which Gunther charges outrageous rents. The massage parlor is in one of those; when Gunther's feeling uninspired, we go there and pretend we have to check on things. Only one of the Victorians—the biggest one, in the worst neighborhood—has its original structure and gets rented as one place, to one party.

Acid Rain, the rock band, lives there.

Now Gunther hits the gravel of Acid Rain's horseshoe

drive going fast, and then jumps on the brake so we slide sideways the last thirty feet to the house. Three old Chevy vans are parked around the drive, all painted with the band's name and logo—a thundercloud with a skull and crossbones in it—and seven huge Harley-Davidsons. In the backyard is a big Doberman and an even bigger shepherd, both on frail-looking chains. They start howling at us. The washing machine and dryer are still out there, their doors torn off, birds and squirrels living in them, and enough old hibachi grills to build a rusty bridge to Barbecueland. Here and there stray concrete blocks and bricks are making dead rectangular voids in the two-foot-high crabgrass.

Gunther loads my arms with equipment from the back of the Bronco—coils of pipe, rolls of solder, garnet paper, a plumber's snake, a portable light, extension cords, a large toolbox. He leads the way with the propane torch, me following him to the house like a pack mule. Luke, the leader of Acid Rain, greets us.

"Why the fuck don't you call your answering service?" Luke says.

"Now, Luke," says Gunther, "I don't think you should be the one to start casting stones. I could say hurtful things to you too. I could say, for instance, why don't you stop trying to flush each other down the toilets? It clogs them up."

"Ha, ha," Luke says. Then he doesn't say anything else, because he doesn't know where Gunther's breaking point is. Luke is not dumb, but you can see in his face that he can't figure Gunther out. He understands that Gunther did not go from being a poor, snot-nosed son of a drunked-up electrician to owning a small real estate empire by taking unlimited abuse from people like him. But then sometimes Gunther seems a jolly fellow who doesn't always act in his own best interest. It's confusing for Luke. I sympathize.

And then there's the way Gunther looks, the massive pink presence of him.

Luke reports that all three toilets in the house are broken. I look at Gunther and narrow my eyes. He looks away, sheepish. On the ride over here, Gunther let slip that Acid Rain first called about their toilet a week ago. It was just the first-floor toilet then.

We make our way through the house. Acid Rain's place was an opulent Cleveland mansion once, and there are still great cut-glass chandeliers hanging in the downstairs rooms above the drums and amplifiers and dismantled motorcycles. The glass pendants are gray blobs now, coated with greasy dust. The residents have decorated the chandeliers with panty hose, pictures from motorcycle magazines, tennis balls, guitar strings. We head upstairs to begin with the topmost toilet. The law of gravity. Various tattooed men are wandering around with women in black leather. Catastrophic metal music is playing in all the rooms on the second floor.

I'd like to mention here that I'm a great lover of music, and so is Tina. We believe that music transcends all the differences between people, and we like to get out when we can to hear a band and dance and have fun. Even after all the things I had witnessed here, we still had perfectly open minds the night we went to see Acid Rain play at the Glo-Worm, over on the other side of the beltway. That's all I can say. When Tina finds out I was here again today, she'll go crazy. Maybe I won't even go home tonight.

Otis, the keyboard player, appears in a doorway on the second floor. Otis is completely blind, and two of Acid Rain's roadies—all the roadies and many other people live in the house with the band—are blind in one eye apiece. People can be blind for many reasons, and you don't ordinarily think of blindness as caused by the blind person, the result of something he did to himself. But with Acid Rain, the thought leaps to mind. Over the months, I've watched to see if other ones become blind too—from drinking rubbing alcohol, say, or fighting among themselves over food or females, the way squirrels do. So far, it's only the same three.

"Is that my landlord?" Otis says. "Do I hear my landlord's voice?"

"My man Otis," says Gunther. "How you doing, Otis?"

"How am I doing? I'm going to the bathroom in the backyard, motherfucker. That's how I'm doing."

"It's under control now, Otis," Gunther says, sidestepping quietly around him and motioning for me to follow. But I'm draped with the coils of pipe, extension cords, the plumber's snake, and I clank when I move.

Otis grabs me. "The dude who mows the lawn, right?" he says. "The landlord's sidekick?"

"I just work for the guy, Otis," I say. "You think it's a picnic? You think he doesn't do the same to me? Every day's a nightmare with this bozo, Otis."

Otis smiles and holds out his palm. "Hey," he says.

I slap his hand. "Renters of the world unite. Death to landlords."

"Right on!" Otis says, slapping me back. "Let's do it now!"

"No, Otis," I say. "Let him fix the toilets first."

"Good point," Otis says. "OK. I'll be waiting right here."

We head up the last flight of stairs. "You overdid it a little," Gunther says, "but I was still impressed. You were convincing, and I liked the way you improvised under pressure. I thought you were just a writer. Now I find out you have natural acting ability. I'm giving you a screen test when we get back home."

On the third floor, Gunther sees the toilet from the hallway. His face becomes an image of the human capacity for sadness. "I think I just got a blown mind gasket," he says. He lights up the propane torch and shoots little bursts of blue flame into the bathroom. "Firing retro rockets," he says. "Leaving doomed planet."

"Two words, Gunther," I say. "Just two little words."

"I know," he says. "You quit."

"No," I say. "Roto-Rooter."

"That's one word," he says. We back away from the bathroom. Gunther grips the banister and looks down into the spacious stairwell as though he might plunge himself into it. Then his head snaps up and he slaps me in the belly. "I just had an incredible idea," he says.

"No, Gunther," I say. "Whatever it is. Please, no."

"Everything just fell together for me," he says. "Oh, man, this is good."

Back down on the landing, Otis is waiting. "Otis," Gunther says. "It's bigger than we thought. We have to call Roto-Rooter."

"You lie," Otis says, producing a length of chain from his leather vest.

"No, Otis," I say. "He's telling the truth this one time. It was my idea to call Roto-Rooter. There's no way this clown can fix these toilets."

"OK," Otis says. "I believe you, brother. But if you lie, I kill you too."

"Don't worry, Otis," I say.

We head downstairs. In the kitchen we find Luke and some of the women swigging on bottles of Colt 45.

"Luke," Gunther says. "My man. I want to ask you a question. You like movies, Luke?"

"I like going to the bathroom," Luke says, slamming his bottle on the table.

"We're calling Roto-Rooter on that, Luke, OK? Roto-Rooter, like on TV? The guys in the big yellow truck with the little sissy uniforms? You'll be able to make poo-poo right here tonight. Now sit down. I want you to answer my question. You like movies?"

"Yeah, sure."

"OK. When was the last time you saw a really great movie about an American rock-and-roll band? I mean a movie that had it all—bar scenes, motorcycle scenes, dressing room scenes, rehearsal scenes, groupie love scenes, and the monster victory-concert scene at the end when the band comes back to its hometown after making it big. A movie that captured all the suffering and the glory, the whole incredible life of a great, semi-famous cult rock band in a medium-sized American city. Luke, when was the last time you saw a movie like that?"

"I never saw no such movie," Luke says.

"That's right!" Gunther says.

. . .

The Peter Pan Diner, 2:00 P.M. Alice comes over with the menus. "You guys really making a big day of it, huh?" she says.

"We're celebrating, Alice," Gunther says. "Two meatloaf specials, one for me and one for my lucky charm here. Gravy on everything. That's the password today, Alice. Gravy."

Alice flashes me a look—can I handle him by myself? I nod and she takes the menus away.

Gunther is on an inspirational roll. "This is it!" he says, gripping my shoulder. "My movie! Plot, characters, myth, fantasy! Commercial potential! It was right under my nose! But that's the way it always is in the art game, eh, Roscoe?" He pulls a legal pad out of his briefcase. "So what do you think? I say we start with the Luke character—let's call him Luke—we start with him as an inner-city kid, you know, getting his first guitar, getting beat on by his alcoholic father because he practices guitar instead of getting a job. Plays good pool and B-ball, but he's better on guitar. Everybody's against him. His fellow gang members think guitar is for queers. And we need the bad father, right? We've got to give Luke something big to rebel against. I mean, he can't *like* his father."

"Cliché, Gunther. Cliché, cliché, cliché."

"You always say that. Well, I say life's a cliché! I'm not letting that stop me!"

"Scratch the childhood," I say. "It begins with music, the band rehearsing in this tenement while the titles roll up the screen. Helicopter shot of the building, close in on the window of their apartment, music getting louder and louder until we're right in there with them. Then the landlord bursts in, demanding the rent. They don't have any money, so they beat the landlord to death with their guitars."

"Sounds like a cliché to me!" Gunther says, chortling and writing it all down. "But it's not bad! We might be able to use that! OK, no childhood. Maybe we can put it back later. Or maybe—how about this?—Luke can go back and see his old dad in the hospital after he's famous. The old dad has the big C in his liver now, but together they watch Luke in concert on the tube in his hospital room. Just before he dies he recognizes how wrong he always was."

"And he apologizes for the way things were. And it straightens Luke's head out about his life."

"Right!"

"Perfect."

"And the record biz, hey? We need a big scene with these parasitic record-producer types who want to tell Luke how to play, what kinds of clothes to wear. They want to make Luke like everybody else so they can use him to get all this money to put up their own noses. But Luke has a dream. He tells everybody to screw themselves. In the end they all want to kiss his ass."

"That's good," I say. "That's original." The meat-loaf specials arrive. We dive into gravy. "Gunther," I say after a few bites, "it takes millions of dollars to make a real movie. You realize that, right? Millions."

"I have a little surprise for you," he says in the nursery-rhyme voice.

"No, Gunther, please, whatever it is, no."

"We're going to my place after lunch," he says. "Hollywood's paying your salary for the rest of the day. Before, I was going to leave you with the toilets and do the heavy business on my own. And I was worried, I admit it, because I didn't have the killer idea to show the big boys. But it came to me when I needed it. We're partners now, Ricardo. I always said you wouldn't be sorry if you stuck with me."

"Big boys?" I say. "What big boys?"

At Gunther's house, a silver Mercedes with vanity plates is parked at the top of the drive. Gunther downshifts the Bronco and creeps toward the silver car as though he can't believe it's actually there. "This is really happening," he says.

For a year now he's been running an ad in the paper to attract investors to his film-production company. Every month a few cranks respond; that's all, nobody with money. But yesterday when he called his answering service he found a message from these guys. They've invested in movies before. He told me about it on the way over here.

He parks the Bronco and gets out. The two men getting out of the Mercedes look like they want to get back in when they see him. The driver is a thin young guy with a spiky haircut, blue-green iridescent jacket, Hawaiian shirt, black jeans, red shoes. The passenger is a small man in his early sixties, salt-and-pepper hair brushed back, business suit. Gunther introduces himself and shakes hands. He motions for me to come over. "Gentleman," he says, "this is my associate, Flip. Flip is the co-author of my new screenplay."

I shake hands too. The driver's name is Willie. He's into the whole sullen James Dean thing. The passenger is Joseph, kindly and soft-spoken, with an Eastern European accent. His voice makes me see scenes for a movie version of our horrible century—bombings and occupations, pogroms, refugee camps, a boy in shabby knickers calling out the prices of fruit on the streets of the New World.

Both men are looking at my clothes. I brush the front of myself, but none of the paint spatters come off. "We like to be comfortable," I say.

Willie licks his lips, dubious, but Joseph smiles and nods. We go inside. Willie and Joseph look around. Gunther's place looks good. It's a big old house that didn't look so good when I first saw it, but often, while his tenants suffer, Gunther has me work around here. I've painted every room, sanded and finished the floors. One week in the winter we tore out the whole kitchen and put in a new one. Sometimes Gunther even has me clean the bathrooms for MaryLou, his wife, while he sits on a hassock in the hall telling me about screenplay ideas.

"You're prospering, Gunther," Joseph says.

"I guess I'm doing all right," Gunther says. He's more nervous than I thought he was. He tries to wink at me but botches it and looks like he's just been poked in the eye. "Flip, would you show Joseph and Willie into the living room? Gin and tonics, gentlemen?"

"Very good," Joseph says.

"Flip? Or would you prefer one of those nice English ales?"

"Gin and tonic is fine, Gunther," I say. I take the men into the living room. The furnishings are trim and tasteful, vaguely Scandinavian. They were chosen by MaryLou. Gunther would have chosen a lot of chrome bars and Naugahyde. The living room makes me realize in a sudden sweet way just how completely MaryLou holds Gunther's life together for him, what an impossible piece of luck or inspiration it was that he married her. If she ever left him he'd have to die, but she never will. She's a loving soul, from people even poorer than his, her head not easily turned from grateful devotion. Gunther put her through college while he worked, and never made it to college himself. She teaches grammar school now and thinks his carryings-on are what you put up with when you're married to a genius.

We sit down. French doors open from the living room into the dining room, now the office of the production company, where the big, useless 16mm Movieola is poised like an old burro grazing among the bundles of screenplay drafts stacked everywhere. I've written whole scenes of them while Gunther's tenants acted out their martyrdom. Joseph and Willie are peering in there from the sofa. They don't know what to make of it all. I hear Gunther clinking glassware in the distant kitchen.

In a voice as soft as Joseph's I say, "Gunther is an unusual person." It's hardly an outlandish statement. They nod, meaning that they'd noticed, and wait for me to go on. "He's actually rather amazing. Four, five years ago he had nothing. Now he owns properties all over town. Everything he has he built up for himself, with no help from anyone. His drive to succeed is unstoppable. All his life he's dreamed of making movies. He works on screenplays in his sleep." I lean forward and lower my voice even further. "His father was an electrician who drank himself to death, beat the kids, and smashed up the house all the time when Gunther was growing up. Now Gunther supports his old mother, bought a nice little house for her to live in across town. He put his wife through college. You'll see him come in here with a Coke for himself. He never touches a drink, straight as an arrow. You understand what I'm saying. I'm talking about character, what motivates a man."

Everything I'm telling Willie and Joseph is true. Yes, I'm casting it in a certain light, even perceiving it as I say it, but I'm not telling a single lie.

"A lot of people have had it tough," Willie says.

But Joseph waves his hand. "I appreciate what you say," he says.

Gunther comes in with the drinks on a tray, three gin-and-tonics and a Coke for himself. He sits down in a big chair. "Well," he says. Then he's about to say something else, but nothing comes out. We sip our drinks, waiting.

"So, Gunther," Joseph says, "you want to make a movie."

Gunther nods without expression. To the untrained eye, he looks as enigmatic as Buddha, full of secret knowledge. But I've learned to read the fantastic face. He wants to speak, but his body has locked up on him. He never really believed that a man like Joseph would come to his house someday. His stage fright is as immense and immovable as himself.

"Joseph," I say. "Willie. Have you ever noticed that beyond the basic animal requirements there are very few things that all human beings must have, and that these few things are not physical but rather metaphysical, things of the spirit? Faith of some kind is the obvious example. Can you think of another?"

Willie looks at Joseph. "This is kind of a weird thing to be talking about," Willie says.

But Joseph thinks it over and says, "Love, of course."

"Oh, good," I say. "Right. The big one. And how about learning, some systematic acquisition of knowledge?"

"Yes," Joseph says, nodding his head.

"Now I'm thinking of one more," I say. "One more nonphysical thing that all people must have, a thing that is always present whenever human beings gather together in grief or in joy."

Willie looks at his watch. Part of his job is to protect Joseph's precious time. "This is kind of like Twenty Questions," he says. "This might be fun at a party."

"Party is a clue," I say.

Joseph straightens up on the sofa. "Music!" he says.

I nod my head and smile. "Yes, Joseph, music."

"The nonphysical part fooled me," Willie says.

"Now, friends," I say, "the movie we're going to make is about music. Joseph, I'll bet there's a tape machine in your car out there. I'm going to guess what's on it at this very moment. Mozart."

"Wrong!" Joseph says, clapping his hands. "Mozart is in the glove compartment, I'll grant you that! But on the machine is Prokofiev. We listened to it on the way over here." He wags his finger at me. "You were wrong, smart boy!"

"Ha-ha!" I say. "But still I've made my point. You take your favorite music with you wherever you go. *And,*" I say, "the second part of my point—it's music that Willie doesn't like."

"Right!" Joseph says. "He complains every day. But that part was easy, smart boy. Look at Willie's clothes, look at his hair."

"Sure," I say. "But look further, Joseph. Look at Willie and see the American moviegoer. We practically have Mr. Entertainment sitting right here. And that, Joseph, is why —for the crucial question—we must now defer to Willie."

I sip my drink.

"Willie," I say. "I have a question for you. When was the last time you saw a really great movie about an American rock-and-roll band? I mean a movie that had it all—bar scenes, motorcycle scenes, dressing room scenes, rehearsal scenes, groupie love scenes, and the monster victory-concert scene at the end when the band comes back to its hometown after making it big. A movie that captured all the suffering and the glory, the whole incredible life of a great, semi-famous cult rock band in a medium-sized American city. Willie, when was the last time you saw a movie like that?"

"I never saw any such movie," Willie says.

"That's right," I say.

Gunther's kitchen, 5:00 P.M. Gunther on the floor on his hands and knees.

"Gunther, get up," I say, looking in the refrigerator for those good English ales he was talking about. "Stop doing

that. Show some self-respect. Where are those ales, you
charlatan, you complete fraud? What if I'd decided to have
one?"

"There wouldn't have been any left," he says, continuing
to do what he's been doing—crawling on all fours, nudging
MaryLou's silver serving tray around the floor with his nose
the way a dog nudges its bowl. Periodically he howls like a
dog too, and when he does, tears spring from his eyes—
which he takes care not to let drip upon the small slip of
blue paper resting on the silver tray.

"I'm making a movie!" he keeps bawling between howls.

The slip of blue paper is the check Joseph wrote to Gunther before driving away in the silver Mercedes ten minutes
ago. It's for an amount so large I can't bring myself to say
it. When he wrote it, Joseph called it good-faith money.
He has more, and he knows other investors.

I finish making another gin-and-tonic. "Gunther," I say.
"I have to tell you something, and I want you to brace
yourself. I'm not doing this movie with you."

He clambers up from the floor, Joseph's check in his
hand. "Flip," he says. "Don't even joke about things like
that, Flip."

"I'm not joking. Where did you get 'Flip,' by the way?"

"It just came to me," Gunther says. "But I like it. That's
you from now on. Flip, my man Flip."

"It's not bad," I say. "But you'll have to find somebody
else."

"There is nobody else! Nobody like you! Nobody with
your talent! Hey! A third of this money's yours! Half of it's
yours! It's all yours, Flip!"

"I already have to go to a marriage counselor on account of you," I say. "If I throw in on this movie, Tina divorces me."

"She won't!" Gunther says. "Not when she hears about the money! I'll talk to her. Call her right now, I'll talk to her. No! We'll bring her in! Can she write? Can she act? Can she sing?"

"No, Gunther. She can't do anything. She's a vegetable now. The only thing she can do is say the word *quit*, over and over. If you ask me again I'm leaving, and I still have most of a drink here." I raise my glass. "Congratulations, pal."

"Thanks, Flip. Flip! We have to celebrate somehow! We have to do something fun together!"

"I can't think of anything, Gunther."

"It's hot out. It's muggy. Flip! You've never been in my pool!"

"I didn't bring my suit today, Gunther."

"You can use one of my suits."

"Really, Gunther."

He pounds upstairs. When he comes back down, he's in his trunks, a total embodiment of what it is to be flesh. He tosses me an extra pair. They're like a hot-air balloon or a parachute. I put them on in the bathroom and come out holding a yard of excess suit behind me. Gunther has the stapler from his desk. He staples the trunks until they stay up by themselves.

We go out the back door and into the yard. Gunther's pool is a big one, with all the fixtures: three ladders, two diving boards, ropes with colorful floats. The blue water sparkles with points of early evening light. "Just a quick dip in the low end here, Gunther," I say. "I have to get home for dinner."

"Flip," he says. "Did I tell you I started taking real scuba-diving lessons? From a registered diving teacher at the Y? He's been showing the class all this neat stuff, special things you have to do in case of emergencies. I have to show you a couple of these things. I can teach you the basics of diving in about two minutes."

"Gunther, no, really. I've always had a slight fear of the water, to tell you the truth. I was swept out into the ocean once when I was a kid, and lifeguards had to save me with a motorboat."

"You never told me that," he says. "That would make a great scene. You should be a little more forthcoming with your experiences. It would help you rise above them." He starts getting the scuba stuff out of the equipment shed. "Now look, these are what we call weight belts. They keep you from floating to the top." He hands me one and starts putting one on himself.

I drop it on the grass. "See you, Gunther. It's been, you know, nice."

He grabs my shoulder. "MaryLou goes diving with me, Flip, and she can't even drive a stick shift. Are you telling me you're afraid to do this? I know, you have to go home. Hey, it's been a special day. I'm asking you to take a little dive with me to celebrate. Ten lousy minutes for a little fun, and then you can go home."

I pick up the weight belt and put it on. Gunther is tying a heavy rope around his waist. About twenty feet of rope is left when he's finished, and he proceeds to tie the other end around me. "Like mountain climbers," he says.

"Divers don't do that, Gunther. No diver ties himself to another diver."

"Yes, they do, Flip. In certain kinds of salvage operations they do. It's a special knot that comes undone when you pull on it." He pulls on the knot and the rope drops off my waist onto the grass. "OK?" He reties the rope for me. "I have this neat maneuver I want to show you—what divers do when one diver for some reason loses his tank or runs out of air. We have to do this particular maneuver if we want to have some fun here today, because I only have one tank with air in it."

"Oh, Christ."

"Put on your flippers, Flip," he says, putting on the only tank with air in it.

I put on the flippers and we slap across the lawn to the concrete apron along the edge of the pool. Gunther explains that we're going to fall into the deep end on our backs, get ourselves oriented under water, and then start sharing the one mouthpiece. I'm going to love it, he says. It'll be much more interesting than simply having my own tank. He shows me how to put the mouthpiece in and out without swallowing water. "Granted, it's a little different up here on land," he says. "Ready? Lower your mask."

I lower my mask. Then, without even giving me a signal, Gunther topples backward like a bomb leaving a plane. The splash he makes comes right over my head like an ocean wave and then the rope runs out and snaps me into the vortex behind him.

Under water it's white and opaque, with millions of tiny

bubbles, and I can't see anything. Then I make out Gunther, his legs and arms wafting gently like seaweed fronds. I watch him swim for a few seconds, fascinated by how graceful he is under water, the way whales are said to be. I can see him smiling around the mouthpiece. He waves goodbye to me as I sink. The weight belt is doing much more to me than to Gunther; soon I'm directly beneath him and panicking. I try to swim upward, but I don't know how to use the flippers and can't kick with them on. I pull on the special knot, but it doesn't work now that it's wet. I try to undo the weight belt, but it's jammed by the rope. I'm about to start crying, despite the unexpected thought that crying under water would be absurd.

Then I feel myself rising toward the surface. Arm over arm, Gunther is hauling me up by the umbilical rope. When he gets me to his level, he pushes the mouthpiece into my face. I'm afraid to breathe through it. *Breathe!* he says with his hands. I breathe. The air from the tank is the most wonderful thing I've ever known, physical ecstasy and my life to do over again. After a few breaths of it I'm all calmed down.

Gunther points to me and moves his arms and legs. *You're supposed to hold yourself up,* he's saying. I point to myself and make some gestures: *I can't.* He gestures, *Try,* takes the mouthpiece away, and lets go of the rope. I try again and sink stupidly, all the way down. He hauls me back up, collects the excess rope, and ties it all into one big bow between us, so that I can't sink too far away.

We fall into a rhythm with the tank, two breaths each time, passing the hose back and forth peace-pipe fashion.

Peace is what it is, an amazing, liquid peace. Each sharing of the air is the deepest cooperation between comrades, something solid and good that would never be withheld. We hear nothing but the gurgling of the tank and somewhere, very distant, the persistent *om* of the pool filter. Random thoughts and memories bubble through me like Aqualung air, one notion after another in bubbly succession, each considered for a globular instant and then allowed to bubble away forever. I've never envied anything Gunther has, but maybe I've misunderstood it all, because I envy this. If I had a lot of money, a swimming pool and a scuba tank would be the first things I'd buy, so that I could leave the earth this way for an hour or two every evening.

A small kick or motion of the arm sends us orbiting slowly around each other in the water like space walkers. Behind Gunther's face mask his eyes are closed. He might almost be sleeping. I see that this is the essential Gunther —who he really is and who he'd be on land, too, if he didn't have to do what he does up there because of what his father did to him.

He opens his eyes and sees me staring at him. He smiles and gestures to the blueness around us as if to say, *Aren't you glad you stayed to check this out?* I nod and give him the OK sign. He points to the surface of the water, shrugs his shoulders, and flops his arms. He actually laughs and a bubble floats out of his mouth with the message, *You really saved me up there.*

I tap my chest, meaning, *I know I did, you huge oaf.*

But the rock-and-roll movie was my idea! he adds, slapping his own chest defiantly. *And I'm not a bad man!* he adds, kicking his feet. *Not as bad as you make out, that's for sure. You're such a judgmental person. My tenants don't need to talk to me about every goddam leaky faucet.*

What about that Pakistani baby? I signal, imitating the mother's flowing robes and jutting out my chin self-righteously.

OK, he nods, *that was wrong, I admit it.*

I make a signal to my heart, meaning, *That really upset my wife. You almost destroyed my marriage.*

He shakes his head with great irritation and lashes his pink fists through the blue water. *Me destroy your marriage! Did you ever think that maybe you shouldn't complain to your wife so much? I'll bet she doesn't bring home every single stupid thing that happens to her every day and inflict it on you. You're such a baby!*

I nod sadly. *OK, you have a point.*

He rolls onto his back and starts paddling both of us around the depths of the pool. I let myself be towed along, staring up at the silvery surface of the water, taking my turns on the scuba tank. The water's surface reminds me of the silver screen of a movie theater, and as a game I try to see a movie in it. At first I don't see anything, and then after a while I begin to see the rock-and-roll movie. I see precisely how it ought to go, what scenes it ought to have, all the things about life that you could make people understand while you had their attention with the music. I see that the world really needs this great, honest, full-of-heart movie about an American band, and that if I don't do it with Gunther he'll screw it up and it won't be the movie I'm seeing. Or Joseph will bring in somebody else to take my place. Somebody else will get to give the world all the pleasure and instruction of the great rock-and-roll movie, and then the world will give that person the swimming pool and scuba tank in return. Why shouldn't it be me?

The text of this book was set in the typeface Avanta
and the display was set in Agency Gothic by Berryville Graphics, Berryville, Virginia.

It was printed on 50 lb Glatfelter, an acid-free paper,
and bound by Berryville Graphics, Berryville, Virginia.

Designed by Chris Welch